WHAT NOW
MY LOVE

FLOYD SALAS

Arte Público Press
Houston, Texas
1994

This book is made possible through support from the National Endowment for the Arts (a federal agency), the Lila Wallace-Reader's Digest Fund and the Andrew W. Mellon Foundation.

Recovering the past, creating the future

Arte Público Press
University of Houston
Houston, Texas 77204-2090

Cover illustration and design by Mark Piñón

Salas, Floyd, 1931–
    What now my love / by Floyd Salas.
        p.   cm.
    ISBN 1-55885-112-7 : $9.95
    1. Narcotics—Fiction. I. Title.
PS3569.A459W48   1994
813'.54—dc20

                                                        93-47654
                                                            CIP

WHAT NOW MY LOVE

1

SHE SLAMMED THE BRASS KNOCKER down on the big oaken door with a solid crack and then waited for somebody to answer. Carole and me, Miles. Her standing in the fourth floor hallway of the apartment house in the Haight-Ashbury district of San Francisco at night and me on the stairway, one step below her. Her in a green chiffon minidress and pale green tights on a pair of long, willowy legs, and me in a pair of brown hiphugger cords and a green turtle-neck sweater. Her six feet tall with long, blond hair that hung clear down to the sweet curve of her ass and me at five-five with black, wavy hair, but lovers, and we both looked hip enough to get into the pad and score some acid.

Footsteps came almost at a trot from the back of the flat right away, then stopped, and the door opened just enough for an eye behind an oblong, Benjamin Franklin spectacle lens to get a look at us, though it seemed to be only looking at Carole, and though I could see through the crack well enough myself to notice the thinning brown hair at the top of some small guy's head, who asked, "Yeah?"

"Sam," Carole said and didn't bother to explain herself, just looked down on the little guy from her full six feet of nineteen-year-old queen, her pale blue eye in profile as cold and glacial as the color of her tow-blond hair.

The eye wavered a little and disappeared, then the door closed and the latch chain rattled and the door opened on this small hippie about my size in a T shirt and hiphuggers, but with the bony body of an old man, who stopped the door when he saw me and started to close it again.

"Hold it! I'm with her," I said, unhappy over having to talk my way into the pad when I didn't want to be there in the first place, and ready to tell him to go fuck himself *and* his acid, which I didn't use, rather than waste my time trying to get inside only to risk getting busted by the heat there anyway.

"Let us in," Carole said and pushed on the door, determined to take me with her, to hip me up a little more, because though she admired my writing and the fact that my first book was coming out in four months and that I taught creative writing at a private college, deep in her, she thought I was sort of square and didn't party with hip enough people.

Still I considered myself a poet, not a playboy, and turned, ready to start down the stairs when the hippie grabbed the door with both hands and frowned at me, but turned back when he stuck his head out on his neck, peered at me from behind his spectacles with the popped eyes of a speed freak, pursed his lips like he was trying to make up his mind, whispered, "O.K." and motioned us by with his head.

Carole was pleased and walked through the short

WHAT NOW MY LOVE

hall and bare front room with long, loose steps and swinging arms, dangling a dark green scarf from one hand in a casual but delicate way that I really dug on such a tall chick, and made me glad I had hitchhiked thirty miles through the rain the night before to make up with her.

But the hippie came bounding by us now and blocked the kitchen door with his body, said, "You can't go in there," and forced us to stop in the front room, which had nothing but a red strobe light shining down on a mattress with a blanket on it, one rocking chair, a portable hi-fi set which sat on the floor, and several psychedelic posters on the walls for furniture.

"Why not?" Carole asked, propping her hands on her hips and looking down on the little cat like she could shove him out of the way if she felt like it.

His oblong lenses sparked with reflections of the red strobe light as if he was angry but his voice dropped down to a whisper again and he said, "Because they're capping in there. Tell me what you want and I'll get it for you."

But Carole called out over his head: "Sam? Get this little bring-down out of the way. He's so speeded up and paranoid, he's about to pop out of his skin."

"She's an old chick of mine, Reggie. Put some music on and let her by," some guy I couldn't see said from the kitchen, and Reggie got out of the way, went over to the hi-fi and started shuffling through some albums, while me and Carole went on through this hall-like pantry into the kitchen, where a dark, dago cat in a white Nehru tunic, with black hair that

3

hung down just over his ears and was cut in bangs across his forehead, nodded to her but kept busy capping the acid in little gelatin capsules with another bearded guy.

He purposely avoided looking at me and acted as if he didn't want to even know my name or anything else about me, and he didn't bother to smile at Carole either, though she was supposed to have been his chick, and I couldn't tell whether it was because of the dangerous scene or because he was just uptight all the time.

"You copped big, didn't you?" Carole said, leaning down to look at the big plastic bag full of blue-colored acid in the middle of the table, popping her eyes out like the little hippie, and I suddenly realized that the eyepopping was a habit that the old pillheads I used to know had. Both speed and benny were amphetamines, and charged cats up so much their eyes literally popped out. Carole had been on a few, strung-out speed trips herself, and it showed sometimes.

"Got three grams and we can count on about eleven- to twelve-thousand caps. How many you want?" Sam asked, lifting his copper-sheened face to her, which looked classically Roman with its high-bridged nose and bangs, and which was almost level with mine, and I was standing up. So I guessed he was about six-three or four easy. But his face could have been cut out of stone and she could have never been his chick, the cool way he looked at her. All he wanted was an answer to his question.

"How much are they?" she asked, her long face as serious as his.

WHAT NOW MY LOVE

"Two-fifty apiece," he said, keeping his cool expression.

"I only want a couple of them, but I'll help you out capping if you want," she said, as if she really had been his chick.

"You want to help?" he asked, speaking to her in a familiar tone for the first time, probably because he was surprised that she'd volunteer, and when I saw how hard they were working to cap the stuff, I understood.

"Yeah," she said and sat down in an empty chair to start helping, which really brought me down. I didn't want to get hung up in any kind of acid factory, especially one that was only two blocks off Haight and three from the Drog Store and all the Hashbury happenings; one which could get busted down in a second. Yet I couldn't bitch about it right away because she was playing her little broad game: making me cater to her for splitting on her a month before, but Reggie came hurrying into the kitchen after putting some album on the hi-fi and said, "Hey! That's my chair!"

"Get another one," Sam said. "She's going to help," and purposely kept his face turned away from me as the first latin, guitar chords of Herb Alpert's "What Now My Love," followed by his simple, swinging trumpet, came on in from the front room.

Reggie grumbled a little but he did it and got another saucer out of the cupboard too, which was about the only dish up there, besides a big platter— all the rest of the dishes were piled, unwashed, in the dirty sink, which looked like a slop pail—then spooned a few tablespoons of acid into it from the big plastic bag, dumped some newspapers off a chair in the corner behind Sam, and sat down to cap.

It looked like a draggy job to me. They all had blue-stained fingers from dipping the capsules into the acid to fill them up, and Reggie missed twice before he got the short half of the capsule into the longer, sheathlike cover after dipping both halves into the acid to fill them up. He then tossed the full, closed cap into a big white bowl in the middle of the table next to the plastic bag. The bowl, with its white scalloped edges, had so many caps in it, maybe three or four thousand, looking as bright and craggy as coral rock, that it resembled a South Sea island shell.

But while I watched Reggie, the third guy with a beard watched me. He was a biker in a levi jacket without sleeves who glared at me like to show me that he could break me in half if he wanted to and had the right to O.K. me being in the kitchen besides. He was a rugged looking cat, too, and seemed to take it for granted that he could whip all the hippies in the room and all at once besides. His cheekbones were sunburned to a chapped red color and wild, brown hair grew out of every part of his face and body, down from the beard into the dirty T shirt that he had on under the levi jacket, and from his matted shoulders clear down to the heavy knuckles of his hands. In fact, he reminded me of a biker who had kicked out a spade cat in front of the Drog Store one Saturday night, who used his boots like a pro boxer uses his fists, put the spade away with four, well-placed boots and almost killed him.

But he was still mistaken about breaking me in

half, by my mind. I went to Cal on a boxing scholarship and though I'm only five-five, and 125, I've got the wiry, flat muscles of a tall, rangy man, with long arms and legs, and I've had over two hundred street fights—though most of them were before I started writing—and won every one, nearly all by knockouts, mainly because I only fight when I have to and then fight with my whole heart, give my life over it, and I'm fast at my light weight but can hit with the power of a big man. So he'd never catch me with one of those kicks, and when he missed, I'd put him away with a single punch of either hand.

Still I didn't blame him for being uptight. The word went down Haight Street like the wind when somebody had a new stash of acid. There'd be pushers on every block, whispering the name of the new brand in your ear when you walked by, some big dealers giving away free samples, and the heat would be by in a few days at the latest. So he better be empty or clean by then or know everybody *he* sold to personally or he'd be busted within a week. I didn't want to be around when it happened either, but couldn't leave because instead of making her buy so we could split, Carole got hungup on the capping and was having so much fun making the illegal dope scene that she teased Sam by pretending to lick the powder off her fingers.

All the guys looked up at her but went right back to working on their caps as if it didn't matter how much she stole with her tongue and Reggie even said, "You'll be stoned in ten minutes on that Blue Cheer, dear, if you lick it, and will probably end up spending the rest of the night in this pad, unable to walk out the door. It's that strong."

"She'll even get high on the air, if she caps long enough," Sam said. "You don't even have to lick it, Carole. Even your friend will get high on the stuff eventually. It turns you on as you breathe. It's aromatic and literally blends with the air. You don't even have to *take* Blue Cheer to get high. It's outta sight. Spread the good word."

He seemed to warm up when I smiled at what he said, looked directly at me for the first time, then cracked his long fingers and commented: "This stuff gets in your pores too. I'm even getting finger cramps."

"Can't you figure out another way to do it?" I asked, willing to be friendly with the guy; but still wanting to get out of there too, I nudged Carole with my knee.

"I could if I had a pill press. But they cost about ten grand, at least, for one without a serial number, that the Feds can't trace," Sam answered, but Carole ignored me, carefully squeezed the two ends of a cap together, threw it into the white bowl and got herself another empty capsule out of a little box.

I nodded to show that I was listening to him but nudged Carole again and got a sullen look out of a slanted eyelid from her.

"Most of the presses don't do too professional of a job anyway," he said. "The pills look like twisted wheels. They're nice though. I had a buddy who had one, but he got wiped out when Superspade got killed. Part of that fifty thou' belonged to him."

"The Mafia wiped that guy out," the biker said,

8

then frowned like he wasn't sure of it, and his eyes were flat and expressionless, like a lot of acid heads I've known who give the appearance of having had too many shock treatments, who can walk and talk and are in contact with whatever is going on around them, but seem to have permanently tranquilized brains.

"Don't be stupid, Hutch," Sam said. "Superspade had at least fifty thou' on him when he got shot and tied into that sleeping bag over on Mount Tam. Almost anybody on the street could have done it. He got killed by the guys he went to cop from, for money. They suckered him in with a good price and then gave it to him. It's that simple. There wasn't any gang war for territory or profits going on."

"Don't get wise," Hutch said, and though he was justified, I had to agree with Sam and felt that much more uneasy being in the pad, especially when Hutch added, "Nobody's going to take us like that, no matter *how* simple Superspade was. I'll blow their fucking heads off with my piece, and that goes for everybody here."

"Shut up," Sam said, looking at me.

"It's O.K., man," I said, "I'm not going to tell anybody. I don't want to get mixed up with guns and acid in any kind of way. And besides, maybe spreading the word around that you've got a gun around can save you some trouble, keep somebody from trying to take it away from you, knowing they might get hurt."

Sam nodded but kept capping, and I was about to nudge Carole again when Hutch, who had been staring at me, said, "Sit down, man. Help out," like he dug the way I looked at things, since it agreed with his. And he was half right. As a former felon, who had had his marijuana conviction wiped off the record after finishing four years' probation, I knew what counted in the underworld: force! But I also knew that I didn't want any part of it, and I nudged Carole again as Sam said, "Why don't you sit down, man," dumped some dirty clothes off a chair by him, pulled it up to the table, and pointed at it. I sat down to be polite, though I had to fight the feeling of apprehension in my chest, which Herb Alpert's smooth trumpet didn't in the least help soothe.

"I know this sounds like a cop-out," Sam said. "But unless you protect yourself from the front, like have a gun and a guy around who'll use it, most of those bikers and spades and all the straight thugs who hang around the street now will try to take the acid away, even if it means killing you. Things really changed in the Hash last summer."

His long fingers trembled when he spoke, like he was really shook up by the violent scene, and I made him for some brought-down idealist, who was disappointed because the "Love Street" had turned out to be—since black market drugs brought such a good price—an underworld complete with murder for gain. But here he was, doing the same thing that he had put down middle-class society for: hustling for profit and backing it up with the force of arms, selling a different product is all.

"Don't hold anybody else responsible for what you believe," I said, but softly so he'd know that I dug his need to defend himself if nothing else. At least the cat wasn't cynical, and I realized that I should have guessed he'd be honest, since Carole had made it with the guy, and she insisted on being right out in front with everything she said and did. Yet, in her rebellion, she stole pretty blouses from department stores and defended it to me on the grounds that the stores were thieving, materialistic institutions, destroying humanity, which I called a lot of shit and said she was a thief no matter what the department stores were.

"True," Sam said, with a humble smile that made me like him and even relax somewhat in the pad for the first time, when somebody pounded on the front door and Reggie jumped up from his seat and rushed out of the room to answer it, and my guts tightened a little, afraid that the first words I'd hear over the tinny sound of the Tijuana Brass would be: "The San Francisco Police Department."

Words could be heard over the bongo drums of the record, and were followed by the sound of the safety latch being unhooked and the door closing, hurried footsteps in the hall, and Reggie came into the kitchen with big eyes saying, "This guy wants to buy a boxful."

He was followed into the room by a tall, skinny hippie with a thick Indian nose and slanted eyelids —wearing a sleeveless Mexican vest, made out of wool, with fancy designs on it—whose sallow skin and long hair and beard made him look like a movie version of a Mormon preacher.

"How much?" Sam asked.

"A thousand dollars' worth," the hippie said. "What kind of deal can I get?"

"Two-fifty apiece."

"Too much," the hippie said, and though there was a drawl to his voice his words were short and final.

"How about two-forty?" Reggie asked, reaching into the bowl and letting a handful of blue caps trickle through his stained fingers, then, dropping his voice down to a whisper, said, "This acid is out of sight, man. Good as the old Owsleys, and that's no put-on."

But the skinny hippie gave Reggie a stern look, like he didn't dig Reggie using his speed-freak expressions to get a better price for his acid, and said, "We've got to make a profit on them, man."

"So do we," Sam said, "and we don't have any trouble selling them for two-fifty."

"I've got a thousand dollars cash on me, which belongs to me and my friends, and I've got to split the profits with them. So give me a good price if you want it."

"Two-twenty-five, then," Sam said and the tall cat chinked his eyes and nodded his head, then pulled a pad and pencil out of his back pocket and went with Reggie into the front room, where they sat down on the mattress and began figuring out just how many caps he was going to get in loud voices that reached us over the record, and I nudged Carole again.

"In a minute, Miles," she said, filling a cap, and I got salty enough to tell her I was leaving, with or without her, when the shriek of an electric guitar being tuned-up vibrated through the flat, ruining

WHAT NOW MY LOVE

Herb Alpert's music, and I asked, "What in the hell's that?"

"The lead-guitar of a rock band who lives next door," Hutch said.

"Jesus Christ, man. How do you stand it?"

Hutch just shrugged his shoulders but Sam said, "I don't mind them when I'm stoned, which is a good part of the time around here. And they're pretty good when they get warmed up. They support their habits off their gigs."

I started to say something else about it but stopped when I barely heard the clap-clap of the front door knocker over the long scream of the guitar, and Reggie jumped up from the mattress and hurried to the front door again. But there was no sound of voices before the door closed this time and several pairs of footsteps came directly down the hall, through the front room to the kitchen.

A small-boned little hippie with a rapier mustache and pock-marked skin then walked in with a little hippie chick and a little child—I couldn't tell if it was a boy or girl because of its long curls—about three years old, sucking on the nipple of an empty bottle and wearing nothing but a pair of cotton trousers and a pair of keds without socks, its bare torso blue-fleshed from the chill in the night air, which brought me down so bad on top of Carole's stalling that I got up to leave as the little cat asked, "How about a free sample?"

Sam reached right into the bowl, held out his hand and dropped two caps into the little guy's palm for an answer. The guy popped one into his mouth first and then gave the other one to the little chick, who turned around and opened the cupboard and seemed to be looking for a clean water glass.

She was a really pretty little chick with tiny points for tits, in a tight-fitting shift, and whose little ass popped out cutely when she stood on tiptoe to search the cupboard. But there weren't any dishes in the cupboard beside the big platter and she started searching through the dirty dishes in the sink and on the drainboard. But the sink was full of dirty pots and other dishes with the dried remains of cooked brown rice still stuck to them, and when she moved a big gray cloth that looked like a dishtowel and caught a whiff of a nasty stink, she dropped it right away, popped the cap into her mouth, turned on the faucet and drank directly from it, without it touching her pretty little mouth, I noticed. She turned around after her drink, then wet her finger, dipped it into the saucer of acid in front of Carole, and stuck it into her little baby's mouth, and Carole said, "He doesn't need that acid. He's already turned on. What's the matter with you?"

"It won't hurt him," her old man with the rapier mustache said. "He'll have a good trip because he's got no hangups to begin with. I believe in turning everybody on, from babies to their grandmothers and grandfathers." And he took his old lady and her baby into the front room to wait for the acid to hit them as Reggie and the skinny hippie with the long beard came back into the kitchen, evidently with the right number of caps agreed upon, and I took advantage of the guitar's and the phonograph's silence and Carole's attention to jab my thumb at the door as a signal to leave. But she only patted my hand and turned away to watch Reggie and the skinny hippie complete the sale.

Reggie went over to an old Victorian slop pail made out of crockery, with some kind of fancy cherub on one side, lifted the heavy lid, pulled out some sheets of paper and said, "There's ten shots to a sheet here, man. We were going to put them out in book form for the dealers to handle easier. You want some of them?"

"Hmmm, yeah!" the skinny cat mused and pulled on his whiskers, then took some of the sheets and began to examine them in his long hands, saying, "Easier to count, too. O.K." And he and Reggie squatted down on their haunches and began to count the sheets, pausing only to hand Carole a sheet when she asked for one.

"How do you get high on it?" Carole asked, and Sam answered, "Chew it. That's how we turned on one of my friends in the county jail."

"Don't read your mail, eat it," Reggie said and smiled at Carole, who said, "Funny nobody thought of that before," as someone knocked on the front door in such a uniform manner that I got scared and listened carefully when Reggie went to answer it, then got more worried when he came back into the kitchen and said in a soft, secretive voice: "There's a guy out there in a fancy Russian shirt who says that he used to cop from the same guy you did in San Diego, Sam. I've never seen him before, but he wants to buy a couple of grands' worth. Should I let him in?"

WHAT NOW MY LOVE

I caught Carole's eyes right away and jerked my head toward the front door and frowned so there wouldn't be any doubt about what I wanted to do, but she crooked her lips in a pained way to put me down for being so rank and threw the cap she had just finished into the bowl, then rolled an empty cap between her fingers to keep from meeting my stare, which got me so mad, that when Sam said, "Let him in. That's a lot of money," I leaned over and said to her:

"Let's get the fuck out of here right now. This place is getting red hot!"

She turned on me then with drooping eyes as if pleading with me not to ruin the groovy ball we had been having for the last twenty-four hours, nonstop, but I insisted, saying, "I'm going to split. Are you coming with me?"

But Reggie came back into the kitchen with the stranger and she used it as an excuse not to answer, and I forgot all about her reply myself when I saw him. At first, I thought I had seen the fancy silk shirt around the street. It was such a brilliant pale blue and had such full sleeves trimmed with lace that nobody would forget it once he had seen it. But it was the guy's round face and fuzzy, golden beard that set the bells ringing in my head. Then I remembered. He looked just like the cat who had set up about fifty surfing hippies the summer before down in Santa Cruz, and every guy in the crowd who was smoking grass in June was in jail by September.

But the guy looked at me too, instead of Sam or all the acid sitting in the middle of the table that he had come to buy, and I turned around to face the sink and pretended to search among the dirty dishes for something as I heard him say to Sam: "I met you once before at Roger's pad in San Diego. Remember?"

"I think so," Sam said but in a doubtful tone, and the guy said, "How many caps can I get for two thousand?"

"You got the money on you?" Sam asked, and the guy must have stuck his hand into his pocket and come up with the cash, because I heard Sam snap the bills and count up to two thousand by hundreds, then say, "Two-fifty apiece," in a strained voice, as if he was either uneasy about making the sale or because the other buyer was in the room and was getting less acid for a better price.

But that was enough for me and, keeping my face turned away from the buyer just in case he *was* the guy from Santa Cruz, I side-stepped in a casual way, like I was just looking around the room, around the table to the dimly lighted hallway that led the length of the flat from the front room to some darkened back bedrooms and maybe some dark back stairs for me to leave by, since Carole didn't seem to want to go and because I was sure that the heat would be watching everybody who went in or out the front door and maybe even taking pictures with infrared film.

My crepe-soled floaters helped me move down the hall with hardly a sound and I glanced through the beaded curtains of the first room, but saw only a window and a closet door in it in addition to the mattress and a floor covered with discarded clothing, books, and cigarette butts. So I moved down to the next room, which was the toilet, and dark too, looked out its window for some sign of some back stairs, saw only the big yellow church, which looked gray at night, across the street, and went on back to the last bedroom, which was also dark and had two windows in it: one which looked out onto the darkened roof of the apartment building next door and Buena Vista Park, which was just on the other side of the building.

The window wasn't locked and gave easily when I tried it, with hardly a sound, almost rolled up by itself once I had first lifted it, and thinking that somebody must have looked out it often, I was even more pleased when I saw that I could stand on a six-inch-wide eave at the bedroom floor level beneath the window and jump eight feet or so across an alley and eight feet down to the next roof, in case of a police raid that is, without having to worry too much about falling the three stories or more to the alleyway between the buildings and busting my skull.

There were also wooden walkways and a wooden deck for hanging clothes on the roof and, better yet, a staircase at the rear of the building with its door open. But I didn't climb out. I went back to get Carole and take her with me out the front door, guessing that there probably wouldn't be a bust right away, though the pad was, of course, being watched, and that so many people had probably been in and out, the heat wouldn't bother to follow the customers but would concentrate on trapping the dealers and anybody else who happened to be around in the house.

WHAT NOW MY LOVE

But I left the window open just in case I had to use it and went back down the hall until I passed the toilet and decided to flush it to give the impression that I had left the kitchen for that reason, in case anyone, particularly the guy in the silk shirt, wondered about it. Then I decided to really take a piss, and unzipped my pants, glanced out the window only because I was standing next to it and saw a gray, unmarked car with its lights off and several men inside pull up next to a row of plum trees on the corner of the little block. I zipped my pants up then with a streak of fear and started to run back down the hall, but checked myself at the toilet door and leaned back to look out the window again and make sure they were cops before I lost my head and panicked.

But sure enough, five men in plainclothes suits and hats got out of the car, closed the door quietly, and started walking toward the apartment house entrance, and I ran out of the toilet and down the hall, not worrying one bit about the noise I made, running toward the little hippie with the rapier mustache and his little chick, who were sitting on the mattress under the red strobe light looking up at me, but turning into the kitchen before I reached them to get Carole and almost running into the agent in the bright blue shirt, who turned white and threw up his arms to protect himself when he saw me and got me so mad I shouted, "You fucking fink!" and brought up a right hook from my side that caught the guy right on the chin, clacked his teeth together, and dropped him flat on his back in the middle of the floor with a heavy thump as I shouted, with my hands up and doubled, ready to fight anybody else who wanted to go too, including Hutch: "The narcos just pulled up in front of the house and are coming in," then grabbed Carole's hand, spilled the cap she was holding, jerked her, open-mouthed and round-eyed, out of her chair, and pulled her into a fast run down the hall after me as a wild, foot-scuffling, shrieking scramble to escape started in the other rooms.

She ran right with me and into the bedroom without balking or showing the slightest fear, and she didn't hesitate either, though she looked perplexed when I said, "Follow me," and threw my leg out the window, hopped over the sill onto the eave, pulled my other leg out the window, then moved over on the eave to make room for her, with my feet turned sideward so as not to slip off.

I watched impatiently, glancing below me for cops, sure one would suddenly shout, "Halt!" and fire at us, while one of her legs arched gracefully through the window, followed by her head, her beautiful hair hanging, Lady Godiva-like, over her face until, straightening up, her weight balanced on the eave, it appeared between the parting strands and was followed by her other leg.

She then stood next to me, holding onto the sill with both hands, looking at me with cool, light eyes, waiting for the next instruction, and I could have kissed her she was so calm, but said instead, "Lean down low so the jump is shorter and follow me. And don't worry. Keep your eyes on the spot you want to land on and you won't miss. Your jump will carry you far onto the roof."

WHAT NOW MY LOVE

Then I crouched down low, leaned as far off the eave as I could while still holding onto the sill, picked a spot on the roof, kept myself from looking down at the sidewalk, three stories below, so as not to get scared, and jumped, caught my breath with a spasm of fear in the air, but landed lightly on the gravel and stood up and waved to her. She leaped immediately, flew down through the air toward me, with her long hair streaming straight up from her head, and landed almost as easily as I did.

"Run!" I said and grabbed her hand and, crouched low, ran across the darkened roof, skirting the chimneys and airshaft, the boardwalks, which would have made our footsteps echo, headed straight for the open door to the back stairs, reached it, jerked her in after me, closed it, and started jumping down the first flight of steps when somebody landed on the roof behind us and a couple of gunshots blasted off.

"Shit!" I said, thinking the heat was either shooting at whoever had landed on the roof after us or was shooting to scare us, though no one had shouted to halt.

But I didn't stop running and, in fact, ran faster, taking the stairs three and four at a time, with Carole following me at the same speed, proving she hadn't worked summers on her uncle's farm in Washington for nothing. But by the second flight the door on the roof banged open and someone started clattering down the steps after us, and I tried to run faster, jumping four and five steps, holding onto the inside rail for safety, with Carole falling a little bit behind me, but both of us gaining on whoever was behind us, and by the time I hit the first floor and ran out

the back door of the building into a narrow walkway, not more than three feet wide, between it and
the next building and started running toward the
street and Buena Vista Park, which was around the
corner from Sam's apartment house entrance, with
lights from windows causing surreal patterns in the
walkway, whoever was following us was a full two
flights behind me, thumping almost cautiously down
the stairs.

Still I kept dashing down the walkway, not dar-
ing to look back for Carole for fear of running into
one of the plumbing pipes or building walls, until I
got to the sidewalk out in front, where I turned and
waved to the dark form running toward me,
crouched low for greater speed, to hurry, and she
had almost reached me when the footsteps thumping
on the stairs stopped and slapped on the concrete
behind her, and I had visions of a cop blasting off
from the dark back there and dropping her between
the buildings before she could get out of the walkway.

But she cleared it and I grabbed her hand and
jerked her into an even faster run across the narrow
street and up a rise on the park lawn, where I
glanced back and saw a tall figure, who looked like
Sam, run by a lighted window and I felt a lot better,
less desperate, though I still wasn't about to slow
down. But Carole glanced back too as we started
down the other side of the rise, saw the guy and
said, "Hey! That's Sam," and started to slow down,
but I jerked on her arm, pulled her almost off her
feet, and rushed down the rise and up the hill around
a big clump of bushes, heading for a horizontal path

WHAT NOW MY LOVE

that cut almost completely across the park. As I
did, I caught another glimpse of Sam through the
bushes standing on the sidewalk looking around for
us, and hoped he wouldn't follow us. But he started
across the street toward the rise too, and I forced her
to run even faster, though my breath was wheezing
out of me and though her breath was heavy and her
face was splotched and her feet were barely lifting
off the lawn on the uphill run.

So I kept going and didn't even slow down when
we passed the kiddie swings and slides between us
and the street and I saw that the window we had
jumped from, with weak, indirect light from the
hall now filling its empty space, had no one in it
looking for us. I thanked God for that small favor
but turned left down the level path that crossed the
park and didn't look back again until we were mid-
way through it, deep in the darkness under some tree
branches that hung over the path, where, still running, I saw Sam pop up behind us, silhouetted by the
streetlights behind him, and then start zigzagging
down the path, calling, "Carole! Carole!," telling
everyone who might be within range of his voice
that he was looking for us.

"This way, Sam! This way!" she answered, and
with my voice hoarse from my heavy breath, I
warned, "Don't yell. You'll bring the heat right
to us," and she didn't shout again but waved when
we ran under a lamppost, and Sam must have seen
her because he called:

"Wait! Wait!"

"Please slow down a little for him, Miles, I can
hardly breathe," she pleaded between pants, and I

ran off the path when it turned uphill, slowed down on a strip of lawn, and finally stopped altogether in some bushes, under some small trees, by a short cut into the park, where I let go of her hand, crouched down in the darkness, panting hard and sweating, but with my lungs and legs in good shape from running seven miles through Golden Gate Park twice a week, and asked:

"Are you O.K.?"

She nodded and leaned against a tree and took deep breaths to get her wind back and barely looked up when Sam came foot-plopping and panting up to us, leaned against the very tree she was leaning against, and, with his head hanging between his up-lifted arms, tried to get his wind back too, and only shook his head when I asked, "Did anybody see you jump from that window?"

He dropped one arm though, and looked at me when I asked him who did the shooting and after swallowing enough breath, answered, "Hutch. He grabbed his gun and went to hold off the fuzz at the door. He had it under the table all the time."

"Oh, no," Carole moaned, and I asked:

"What about the undercover cat in the bright shirt?"

Sam smiled and gave me a nod of respect. "He was still lying there on the floor where you dropped him when I grabbed his money off the table and ran after you guys, saw you going out that window, and thought you were completely spaced out when you jumped, until I saw you run through that roof door."

He stopped then, took a few more breaths, let

both hands slap against his sides, and asked, "How did you know that hippie was the Man, dad?"

"I was down in Santa Cruz last summer when he set up about fifty guys. At least that's what I thought he did, and when the fuzz pulled up in the plain car, it was enough proof for me."

"But what did you hit him for?" Sam asked and leaned down to see my face in the darkness.

"I don't really know," I said, annoyed with myself for falling into an old underworld habit, which I thought I had kicked after I started writing in jail and finally quit fighting altogether, namely, blasting out every guy who either finked on me or burned me so the word would spread how bad I was and keep other guys from making the same mistake. Which got me a good rep but got me into serious trouble too, additionally charged with felonious assault for almost killing a dealer who set me up once. "Maybe I did it to help me get away. But whatever the reason, I'm in for it now. That hippie agent recognized me too, that's why he got scared, and he knows my name and where I teach, everything. The heat will never let up until they get me again."

"Awh, you're in trouble then too," Sam said and Carole leaned away from the tree in surprise.

"The trouble'll be worse for all of us if we don't get out of this park. They know somebody went out that window by now, and they're liable to surround the park and search it with about twenty cops in about a minute," I said, trying to stop the conversation about me, and standing up, I grabbed Carole's hand and started down the short cut, through the bushes, to the street, stopped before I crossed it though, to check for any kind of car light while I could still hide, then headed uphill to the cobblestoned dead end of Waller Street, intending to cut down it the couple of blocks to Carole's pad and my fastback MG, and I said, when I noticed that Sam was coming with us: "We ought to split up," not calling him by his name because I didn't want him to even know mine let alone get familiar with me.

But he got on the other side of Carole, kept walking with us, and asked, "Do you have a car, man?"

He turned his beardless face to me, looking as innocent as a little boy, but I wasn't going for any con, and I only nodded for an answer to discourage any plans he might be making for using my car to get away with, keeping my face as hard and expressionless as I could, hoping he'd get the message and split, but he asked, "Where is it?"

"Not in front of your house, that's for sure," I said, glad that Carole and I had walked across the park to score because of the mild March night, and I started taking longer steps up the sidewalk to get away from the guy, not wanting him around for no other reason than that he had been Carole's guy before me, let alone because he had the two thousand dollars of marked money on him. *All* money the Man buys dope with is marked. But Sam hurried up the steep sidewalk to get in front of me and said, "My point is this. If the Man recognized you, then you've got to get out of town too, right?"

"That's right, daddy," I said and stepped around him. "My career as a college teacher of creative writing is now over."

The ring of bitterness in my voice caused Carole

to turn sharply toward me, as if she thought I was
blaming her for my ruined life by insisting that I go
with her to score, and she pulled her hand free of mine
when we turned down the very steep sidewalk next
to the cobblestoned dead end of Waller and had to
break our speed with our heels to keep from falling,
and though she kept up, she wouldn't look at me.

"Well, look then," Sam said, forced behind us by
the narrowness of the sidewalk, pausing between
words as he rushed to keep up yet keep his balance,
"I've got over two thousand dollars on me, and
you've got a car, and we both have to get away. So
why don't we go together?"

"I don't think that will be very cool," I answered,
without bothering to look at him, and checking
quickly at the corner for car lights, jaywalked across
Waller to the cover of the buildings on Carole's side
of the street, trying to cut off the conversation too.

Sam hurried after me, puffing across the street, and
though I was breathing hard, I had caught my second
wind when we rested, and I speeded up the pace to
get into Carole's pad and off the street before some
alerted cop pulled up and arrested us, and Sam
breathed even harder, trying to keep up and talk too.

"Listen, man. I've got some friends down in
Mazatlán with a camper, and they'd put us up until
we got settled. They'd help us get out of Mexico too,
if that was necessary."

But I crossed Divisadero without even answering
him, hoping he'd give up and split before we got to
Carole's pad and he followed us in, bringing all his
heat with him. But as soon as we got on her block
and I could see my little, green MG parked diagon-

ally to the curb on the steep hill in front of her big Victorian pad, with the beautiful spiral staircase out in front, and I started to believe that I could still get out of the city without getting busted, Carole said, "Why don't you go with him, Miles?" and stopped me in the middle of the sidewalk.

The streetlight shone down on her, giving an electric shimmer to the long strands of her blond hair, a soft sheen to the flimsy material covering her breasts, which rose and fell sensuously with her heavy breathing.

"Go with him and I'll go with you, Miles. Come on, man."

"You'd go with me?" I asked.

"Yes," she said and grabbed my shoulders and smiled, making me want to kiss the sensual bend of her lips, but I pulled away from her, said, "No. You don't have to go," and hurried down the block to her apartment house, where I started running up the spiral staircase to get off the streets and into her flat where it was safe, then make my plans for getting out of the city.

But she chased me and asked me to wait and when I wouldn't she ran up the stairs behind me, saying, "But I want to go, Miles. I want to go."

"Stay here. Don't be a fool," I said, turning my head to see her, but still moving. "They don't even know who you are. Just stay off the streets for a while and keep out of this. It's big trouble."

"But I want to go to Mexico with you, Miles. I want to go," she said and grabbed my pants leg and stopped me. "I want to go with you. We could have some fun. I'd be good company and you wouldn't be alone. You wanted me to go to Europe with you in the fall after your book came out. Well, I'll go to Mexico with you now, not Europe later. I've got four hundred dollars in my room besides. And you won't be responsible for my going, Miles. I swear it."

She was still holding onto my pants leg and looking up at me with a droopy-eyed plea on her long face.

"I don't know," I said, really starting to consider it, and she smiled and ran up the stairs past me as if I had said yes, and she made it up to the fifth floor and her flat so fast that she was already stuffing clothes into her knapsack, which was hanging on the closet doorknob, when Sam and I walked into her unfurnished room.

"I don't know, Carole," I said to stop her and give myself time to think. There was only a red bulb burning in her room and I could see out her tall, uncurtained windows really well, and the sight of most of the Fillmore district lit up below us and a couple of Bay Bridge towers showing just over some brightly lighted city peaks made me sad, knowing that I might not ever see them again. It also made me long for her company on a run that was going to be mighty miserable and might last for years, ending with either jail, my death, or enough success from my book to make the heat finally leave me alone. I knew because I had run before and for grass too.

She sensed my sadness because she stopped packing after she had pulled her sleeping bag out of her closet and had thrown her wallet into the knapsack, and she walked over to me by a window, curled one arm around my neck, touched my face with her fingers, and said, "I really like you, you know. And that's a lot for me to say. I haven't said it to any guy since I was sixteen, and he broke my cherry."

She kissed me then, lightly, but with moist lips, and pleased with the way she acted toward me in front of Sam, I put my hand on her breast, felt the flesh under the filmy material, since she wore no bra, then pulled away from her and said, "O.K. There's no reason to stick around anymore. My family would probably turn me in if I went to them for help. You're all I've got. Let's go. But be sure to bring your money. We're going to need it."

She pecked me on the mouth once more, turned and smiled at Sam, then reached down, picked up her knapsack, slung it over her shoulder, minidress and all, and said, "Let's go!"

2

WHEN WE HIT THE FREEWAY, HEADED
south on 101 a little after midnight, my main intention was to hit the Mexican border between San
Diego and Tijuana as soon as possible, which would
be around noon, figuring on twelve hours of driving,
most of it all night, and I kept my purring MG right
on the speed limit at sixty-five, checked out on the
gas, which was half full, and the oil pressure and
water temperature, which were fine, made mental
plans to get the car refueled and some coffee for us in
San Jose, which would carry us almost to Los Angeles in my twenty-nine-miles-to-a-gallon car, and
made up my mind to keep moving. Because even
with the best of luck in driving, they still might put
out an escape bulletin on us and catch us at the border anyway. Though I did feel better because we had
gone to my pad, picked up my duffel bag, half-filled
with clothes, my typewriter, briefcase with manuscripts, a few books, my sleeping bag, and got out of
the city without being grabbed.

Carole was more than relieved, she was happy, and
she smiled at me and laid her long arm around the

back of my bucket seat, rested her hand on my left shoulder as if she were sitting right next to me instead of way over there in her own bucket seat, separated from me by the gearshift box, and said, "Smile, Miles."

Which I did while I watched Sam in the rear view mirror move things around in the small space in the tiny back seat, put my sleeping bag on the floor next to Carole's, stretch his long legs out over them— though his knees touched the ceiling—and lean his head back over the seat and rest it against Carole's knapsack in the fastback window, with the rest of our stuff, then clasp his hands over his chest and close his eyes like there was nothing more to worry about. Which brought me down. That kind of attitude when we were red hot could get us busted. So to bring things out in the open and wake them both up to the fact that the trip wasn't any party, I said, "How much money do you have, Sam? The exact amount."

"Do you want to know now, man?" he asked, opening his eyes but frowning.

"You fucking A, I do," I said, maybe a little too hard because Carole looked at me.

But Sam sat up enough to reach into the pocket of his cords, pull out his wad of bills, and start counting, though he looked uncomfortable with his head bent against the ceiling.

"You too, Carole. Tell me how much you've got exactly."

"How about you?" she asked, and, stretching, reached completely across the back seat to her knapsack for her wallet, making Sam move a little, but jerked her hand right back out without it when I answered, "Fifty-four dollars."

"Fifty-four dollars?" she said, popping her eyes out like Reggie. "Is that all?"

"That's all, baby," I said. "And that's why I'm asking. They only pay part-time instructors a hundred dollars a month a class, and though I've got nine hundred in the Bank of America, which is half my advance on my first novel, I'll have to send for it from Mexico, when it's safe, and that will take time. So now you know why I asked."

"I can carry us till then, don't worry," Sam said. "I've got twenty-one hundred and sixty, counting the two thousand dollars the agent gave me, and—"

"With my four hundred and something, we've got twenty-five or twenty-six hundred, and that's enough," Carole said, and I didn't get to answer that twenty-five hundred was enough for only a few months with three people living on it because some stupid asshole in a big American car came flying up behind me at eighty with his brights on and forced me to move over into the middle lane, which was empty, to let him pass, and angered by him, I said, "Well, you guys need my car and I need your money. Until we get to Mexico, that is. Where you can split on me, if you want to."

"If we want to?" Carole said and leaned back against her door to look at me. "What are you talking about?"

"About what is. That's all, baby. Facts," I said, trying to get hard so I wouldn't be disappointed later.

"You call the low opinion you have of my prom-

ise to you a fact?'' she asked and waited for my
answer, with her whole face in shadow near the roof
of the car. The dissipation circles that sometimes
showed under her eyes, giving her a sorrowful
appearance, I now felt responsible for, but I said:

"When the Man is after you, everybody cops out
to save themselves. And even the people who can't
be busted with you turn fink on you, and that includes everybody you know: your friends and your
whole family—wife, son, dad, brother, everybody.''

"How can you say that? At the beginning of our
living together?'' Carole asked and looked back to
Sam for support, and I saw him switch his eyes
toward her in the rear view mirror, though he kept
his face fully turned toward me because he knew I
was watching him, then slide his hand across the back
of her seat and touch her lightly on the arm, which
I saw out of the corner of my eye. She acknowledged
it with just the slightest lowering of her head, as if
she might be swallowing even, to signify a nod, and
I got salty. But I didn't say anything about it, decided to watch and wait and see if anything was
going to develop from it. Yet I felt too misunder-
stood and sorry for myself to keep totally quiet, and
I said:

"I'll tell you how I can say that! Because I've been
through all this before. When smoking pot wasn't
the middle-class thing to do and girls who did were
considered bums!''

Carole lowered her eyes with the implication, but
I was angry enough not to stop and said, "You've
never been on the lam before, baby. I have. I tried
to score some grass down in West Oakland one time

when most college kids didn't smoke it, and you had to go down into the underworld to get it. The narcos saw me and chased me up the wrong side of Adeline Street for two blocks but didn't catch up until I had thrown the grass out the window, and I thought I got away with it. But that was the beginning of a long five year run from them up and down California and even down to Mexico City, where they still didn't let up, and tried to set me up every way they could, and finally got to my family through my brother-in-law, and finally even to my wife, until there wasn't a person in the whole world who didn't try to help them bust me. Finally, when they took all the love I had in the world away, I turned myself in. But when I got out my wife no longer loved me, and that's where it's at."

Her long face looked crooked and out of shape, she was so unhappy, but I couldn't stop because I had never told anybody about it before and it flooded out of me: "Just wait until the cross comes down and the Man catches us, and you'll see how quick you want to stick with me for punching a narco agent in the mouth or how long you'll want to stand by Sam when they bust him for sales and possession and unlawful flight to avoid prosecution, for having a whole flat full of dopefiends and guns."

She opened her mouth and took an intake of breath to say something but I beat her to it, almost shouting, "And what if it's murder? What if the biker killed somebody? We heard gun shots, remember? And your being there makes you an accessory? What will you do then? If your life is at stake? Cop out as state's witness, that's probably what. And I won't blame you either. Remember that! I'm just letting you know where it's at so you won't be surprised when this outlaw life up and slaps you in the face."

The car had drifted a little out of its lane on a long curve and I had to pay attention to my driving but I could still see the way her mouth hung open and her head tilted as if I had shocked her so badly she couldn't even talk. But Sam said, "We still don't have to cop out on each other," from so close behind me that he must have been leaning forward all the time I was shouting. "I don't believe we have to. We're not your conventional family that has to co-operate with the police because they lead such a straight life."

"Don't you have any faith in people at all?" Carole asked, finally speaking, her mouth crooked in an ugly manner.

"Not since I lost my wife, I haven't," I said. "She belonged to the Man, not me."

"Well, I'll never cop out, not even if they try to send me away. I hate cops. They're fascist pigs. I don't care what your wife did!" Carole said, her blue eyes hard. But I said:

"I only know one person in my whole adult life who's ever done that."

That stopped her for a moment in which she and Sam looked at each other. Then she asked, "Who?" and when I tried to think of a way to answer without sounding like a braggart, she said, "You?"

"Yes," I said, softly, and got back into the fast lane, wanting to forget the whole thing by concentrating on my driving now that everything was out in front where it belonged, without that sentimental bullshit about hanging tough with a tight mouth when the Man had everybody locked up and wanting to die. Because that's where it was at. I had been there. But when I switched lanes, I noticed the bright lights of the San Francisco International Airport on my left and got unhappy at how small a distance we'd traveled since we hit the freeway, were barely past South San Francisco, and how far we still had to go, with lots of time for still getting into trouble, and I yelled at Carole when she asked:

"What makes you so special? Why are you so uncorruptible and honorable and nobody else?"

"Because I believe in myself, that's why! Even if nobody else does!"

"You know, huh?"

"Listen," I said, lowering my voice, and keeping my speed steady at sixty-five. "Just like I told Sam at the pad. You can't hold anybody else responsible for what you believe. I found that out the hard way. When nobody I knew in the whole world loved me enough to tell the truth in court about how the cops had broken the law by tapping my phone, waking me up in the middle of the night with nobody on the other end of the line, by tailing me, getting me fired from every job I got, and finally throwing me in a psychiatric ward when I turned myself in, and using the psychiatrists to convince me that if I wanted to get out and not spend the rest of my life in a nuthouse, I'd better wake up to the fact that it was grass that was making me paranoid, not cops. I realized then that if I really believed in the things I said I did, then I had to live up to them myself, no matter what anybody else did. That's why."

I ended on a low note, running out of breath, but wanting both of them to know that I was straight, that I did believe in the things they said they did, even if I didn't have any faith that they'd live up to them, and I checked the gas tank again and the water and oil gauges and the speedometer too, to keep from getting pulled over for speeding and maybe tossed in jail, hoping they'd both stay quiet, when Carole said, "Since I don't have anybody else's word for it but yours, why *don't* you cop out like everybody else in the whole world? Why? Why do you insist on not finking when it's made you lose all faith in people?"

I sighed when she said that and sort of braced myself in my bucket seat, with both hands on the wheel, my right foot on the gas pedal, my left leg bent next to the bucket seat to prop me up, and answered, "Because I want to be a free man, first of all. I want to live my ideals, not talk about them and do something else like nearly all people do, and that includes most writers, and especially institutionalized professors, who talk big and act small, play their campus power politics, play it cool when the pressure's on. And secondly but related, I want to be a great writer. E. M. Forster, who wrote *Passage to India*, said once that he hoped he had the guts when the time came to betray his country before he betrayed a friend. And I believe that only a man *that* free will ever produce anything great and original, because he has a unique viewpoint of the world. He doesn't belong to and share the view of life of other people. And any writer, any artist, who helps the oppressive forces of the police to watch, trap, or punish other people, shares the values of those cops, and if he does, he'll never break through the barriers of convention to a cosmic view of life. He'll never say anything new. Because he's a conformist who follows the crowds, who believes—no matter what he says he believes—in the crowd's view. Great art can only come out of an unfettered personality, a person willing to stand totally alone in the world without God or man or love or any crutch but his own conscience. I want to produce great work, and I'm willing to die in the attempt, since I'm going to die anyway. That's why."

"And that means that only great people don't cop out?" Carole asked, and when I only nodded my head for an answer, since I was tired of talking about it, she must have taken it for smugness, because she shook her head and wrinkled her nose and said, "You're a real bring-down, Miles. You're really cynical. You make it almost impossible to have a real relationship with you. What'd you let me come for, if you didn't want me with you?"

"I do want you with me," I said.

"You don't talk like it."

"I want it. I'll risk on it. I'll take a chance with you, because I need you. I dig you. But that doesn't mean that I think our scene will last under these circumstances. I don't have any illusions about what's up ahead there on that dark highway, baby. And I don't want any. I only believe in the here and now as far as people are concerned. Fuck the past and let the future take care of itself, because it will anyway. There's only going to be two kinds of joy on this trip and that's writing good everyday and having a fine broad to love and be loved by.

That's why I'll take a chance on you. But I won't cry for long if it doesn't work out."

She sat as far back in her seat as she could then, as if she didn't want to be contaminated by me, and shook her head with disgust once more, but I could tell by the slight switch of her eyes that Sam had touched her sleeve again, and I felt that it was all useless, that none of it was worth the misery of going on the lam again after five years of it, with all its unpleasant and frustrating complications, the alienation from everything and everyone I loved. And I suddenly became extremely conscious of my body and its place in the car, on the freeway, in the middle of the whole landscape, that part of the earth where I happened to be. I could feel my weight sagging down in the bucket seat, the hump of my back against the backrest, the edge of the seat under my knees, the tongue of the gas pedal under the ball of my right foot, the hum of the gearshift in my right hand, the rasp of the tires on the bad freeway paving, the vibrations of the car's body in the steering wheel, and got so depressed by the flat, dreary land around me with its wire-linked fences, back walls of factory buildings, motel and rat exterminator signs, drive-in theaters with names on marquees I never bothered to read, that all I could see up ahead where the freeway faded into blackness was a bleak, bleak future for me.

3

WE REACHED THE WIDELY LIGHTED SAN
Jose area about one o'clock after a lonesome hour's
drive down the dark peninsula in which none of us
spoke and Sam didn't play fingertouch with Carole
the whole time. But when I pulled off the freeway
into a service station, which was the only business
open on the outlying street, to get the tank filled and
the water and oil checked, and asked the young,
brown-haired attendant where I could get coffee to
go and only got a shake of his head before he went
back to fill the tank, Carole said, "I don't want coffee. I want to get high."

She was sitting up against the door again, with
her legs crossed, the knee of one leg half-way up the
backrest of her bucket seat. Her leg was so long that
its toe disappeared under the dash. But when I didn't
remark on what she had said, she asked Sam: "Do
you have any grass?"

"Not me," he said, shaking his head. "The only
thing I took out of that house was the money. I
haven't had any grass in about a week. I don't get
high much when I'm dealing."

She looked at me then with the same question on
her face, though she wouldn't ask it, and I said, "Not

me either, baby. I haven't had any in a couple of days myself."

"Shit!" she said and slumped down in her seat, and Sam said:

"I can probably score some in L.A., if that'll make you feel any better. I've got friends in Venice who'll probably lay a few joints on me, make our trip to Mexico from there real groovy."

"No it won't," I said, coming on too hard again and knowing it.

"Why not?" Carole asked so loudly that I looked around to see if the attendant had heard, and though he seemed to be preoccupied with filling the gas tank, there was a frown on his tanned face and wrinkles around his eyes which gave him an age that the rest of his smooth, nineteen-year-old face didn't have, like he had worked since he could get a job and it showed, but which made me fear that he had heard our conversation, and I said, very softly to quiet her without drawing attention to it:

"I don't want to take a chance on getting hungup there. Lots of things could happen in Venice. It's always hot and we might get busted. And once the San Francisco heat gets enough information to identify us with, they might put out an escape bulletin on us and catch us either in Venice or the border if we don't get across fast. The best thing to do is get out of the country right away. We can score in Mexico if we want to."

"What difference is a few minutes in L.A. on a Sunday morning going to make?" Carole demanded loudly and uncrossed her legs to twist around and face me better, showing me her pale green thighs clear to her crotch. I put my finger to my mouth to warn her to hold her voice down, then answered:

"A lot. It might take a few hours, and it might even take a couple of days, maybe a week. You know how scoring grass is, unpredictable. And it only takes a couple of hours to get from L.A. to TJ, and I'd rather get across first. That's the difference."

She was still but pouted and the irregularities of her features showed, the bump on her nose. the unusual length of her face, but especially her mouth, which looked crooked, as if she might be biting the inside of her lip and though she was still striking with the light from above the gas pumps filtering through her blond hair, silvering her skin, she was almost homely.

"It probably won't take me long to score in L.A., Miles," Sam said, calling me by my name for the first time, leaning on the back of my seat, his head pressed up against the ceiling.

"No," I said, raising my voice I was so angry at him for trying to con me. "I'm not going to stop and take a chance on getting busted just to get somebody high!"

But I said it much too loud and the attendant, who had set the gas hose to stop by itself and who was now in front of the hood waiting for me to pull the release so he could check the oil, stared at me hard, and even glanced at me again after he propped the hood up, then once more when he held up the oil gauge to check it, but kept his face turned when he put the water in the radiator because he knew I had seen him, though Carole said, loudly, as if she hadn't even noticed him: "You've got this puritanical gravity that brings me down, Miles. None of my friends is like that and you don't like my friends," then glanced back at Sam, and I shouted:

"It isn't a matter of your individual friends. It's the scene! The crowd! That's the trouble! Look at us now!"

She blinked and shut up but gave me such a hard look that I wanted to explain myself more clearly, justify myself so she'd understand. But the attendant came over to my side of the car to wipe the windshield and kept glancing through the glass at me and I had to keep quiet, though I did get a look at his bony face and hard little brown eyes, his brown hair pomaded back, grease on his thick-fingered hands of course, and I disliked him as much as he disliked me, but was determined to keep quiet and play it cool even when he walked around the front of the car to get Carole's window, and she asked, "Well? What about L.A.?"

"Hell no. It would be stupid to stop only a couple of hours away from TJ, where we can score all the grass we want and be relatively safe besides," I said, and she didn't get a chance to argue because the guy started wiping off her window and was busy catching glances at those green-clad legs through the glass until he saw me watching him and started wiping with brisk, circular strokes to show how conscientious he was and to finish quickly too. But he was so annoyed at me that he frowned and kept frowning when he put the cleaning spray away and went back to finish filling the tank.

She turned to stare at me then with brittle blue

eyes and nodded openly to Sam to thank him when he touched her, slightly, on the arm again, and I said, "If you need any reasons for my distrustful attitude, think about your little finger-tapping game with Sam here," and he froze with his fingers still touching her arm.

"I'm going potty," she said quickly and opened her door and got out, seemed to shoot up to seven or eight feet and out of sight as she stood up, then strode past the gas pumps and around the corner of the building to the women's head.

"Me too," Sam said and got out himself, walked out of sight around the building too, leaving me with the bitter satisfaction of having made them run at least, which was a small consolation I lost quickly when a highway-patrol car pulled into the station and up to the gas pumps on the other side of me, facing the same way.

He said something to the attendant, could have been just a hello, and smiled as if he knew him. The attendant put away the gas hose quick though and went over to the cop's window, where he stood with his back to me and said something in a very low voice. The cop peeked around him at me, then said something in a very low voice back, and the attendant came around to my window.

"Three-eighty," he said, his voice quavering he disliked me so intensely, and couldn't keep the frown off his face even when I handed him four one-dollar bills with a smile. He then went to the cashbox, unlocked it, but said something to the cop when he was making change, and the cop moved his car up almost parallel with mine so he could see me more clearly and stared at me with that cold-eyed look used by all cops when they're working, even when they're in plainclothes and don't want you to know they're heat. And aware of his harsh, straight features, I had to look away without being too obviously intimidated, or he'd think I had something to hide.

I sat in the car trying to play it cool, acting as relaxed and unconcerned as possible, afraid that the attendant had mentioned dope to him and that when he saw Sam with his Prince Valiant haircut and Carole in her minidress, he might decide to shake us down, and Sam's money *could* get us busted, for investigation at least. Then when the attendant came back and stiffly laid the two dimes worth of change in my hand and gave me another dirty look out of his little brown eyes, his bottom lip so taut with hatred it was almost quivering, I was really sorry that I had lost my temper as usual and brought the heat down on myself, though there wasn't too much I could do about it.

The cop even pulled his car up a little more so he could get an even better look at me, since I had turned my face away, and I could see the black hood of his patrol car out of the corner of my eye. I then glanced at him in a naturally curious way, full-faced, but he had already turned his face in the other direction to watch Carole and Sam walk back from the rest rooms.

Sam faltered when he saw the cop car, dragged out a step, then pressed his arms to his sides and walked with stiff-legged steps past the headlights, his features tight and worried, and even had trouble squeezing into the back seat, he was so tense.

46

"I've got that marked money on me, man," he whispered so suspiciously I was afraid the bull would shake us down right then.

Carole was almost past the patrol car when I saw her, Sam had blocked my view so completely getting into the back seat. Her long legs, illuminated in the pale tights, were carrying her at a relaxed glide past the headlights, and when she opened the door and got in, she stuck one leg in first and sat down, letting the other bent leg stick way out so that her legs were spread clear to the crotch and the copper could get his kicks if he wanted to, though she had probably outraged the guy, he was frowning so badly. His frown worried me some, but I still had to admire the relaxed way she acted. He was the one who was uptight, not her, and he could never accuse her of acting suspicious and get away with it.

I had the car started before she pulled her leg in and in gear before she closed the door, and I pulled quickly but carefully out of the station, turned left, back toward the freeway, which was a couple of blocks down the darkened street, and didn't get a half a block down before the cop car pulled out of the station too and the bull began to follow us.

"Carole, turn around like you're talking to me and keep your eye on those headlights following us. there's not another car on the street, you won't have any trouble. But not you, Sam. He might see your face through the back window, even if it is full of our stuff," I said, trying to keep him from turning around, but he must have looked anyway, because he cried:

"Hey, man! He's catching up on us!"

"Split on him, Miles," Carole said.

"There ain't no splitting on him. If I drive faster, he'll stop me for speeding. Is everybody clean? Double-check," I said and watched Sam in the mirror pat his pockets down, pull out the wad of money, and ask:

"What shall I do with this?"

"Give it to Carole, man. And you, Carole, you put it in your tights. He can't search you down there. Only a female bull can do that."

Sam shoved the wad of bills between us and Carole took it, flipped up the front of her minidress, jammed it down in the crotch of her tights, and snapped the skirt down as the cop car started coming up fast in my side view mirror. I kept my speed up to thirty miles an hour, taking advantage of the extra five-mile leeway over the speed limit that most traffic cops give a motorist, and tried to squeeze out a lead on the tiny pair of headlights in the mirror, while I kept my eyes on the black and white freeway sign up ahead which read: "101 SOUTH, LOS ANGELES."

"Hey, man! He's coming up fast," Sam said.

"Keep cool," I said, noticing the calm way Carole sat turned in her seat so she could see out the fastback window, her face fine and sharp, her slender brows nearly touching between her eyes, and her silence even when the cop's red light went on and he gave us a blast of his siren.

"The sonofabitch. He didn't need that siren," I said and pulled over next to an empty lot, only a few feet from the freeway entrance, then braked to a complete stop, let out a big breath of air, said,

"Everybody play it cool. We're just going down to L.A. for a few days," and rolled my window down, as if there was no cause to get out of the car.

The bull pulled up behind me, got out, came straight to my car with his flashlight in his hand, pointed it at me, caught my eye with the reflection of the red spotlight in it a fraction of a second before he turned it on, and blinded me. I ducked my head and blinked my eyes and was still trying to get the moons out of them when Carole said, "Hey! Get that light out of my face! What is this?"

"Let me see your identification," he said, in a very official tone, his face down close to mine so he could see her, and I was surprised at how wrinkled it was. It was so lean I thought that he was a young man back in the gas station, but he was in his late forties, maybe fifty easy.

"Get that light out of my face so I can see and I will," Carole said, and I was worried she'd get him mad enough to bust us. But he ignored her and switched the light beam on Sam, who sat back stiffly and squinted his eyes at the glare.

"What's your name?" the cop demanded, but before Sam could answer, I asked:

"What's this all about?"

But the bull just shone his light back in my face and asked, "Where you from?"

"San Francisco and headed for Los Angeles. I'm a professor at a college up there. I'll show you my faculty card," I replied, pretending to be annoyed, and he lowered his light a little as I pulled my card holder out of my back pocket and handed both my faculty card and my license to him.

He looked at each of them carefully under the cone of light, his sharp face peaked and cold, but then asked in an almost decent tone: "What do you teach?"

"Creative writing."

"Do you have any other proof of identification?" he asked, the glow from the red spotlight giving one side of his face a heated, angry look.

"Isn't that enough?" I asked, curtly, and Carole leaned against me and reached out the window with her passport.

"Here's mine, if you need anything else," she said, and the bull took the passport but flashed the light in her face again.

"Get that light out of my eyes. Who do you think you are?" she said, and I held my breath, expecting him to order us out of the car.

It looked like he was, too, the way he kept the light on her face and forced her to lean back in her seat to get out of its beam, but he answered, "It's in the line of my duty to check the identities of suspicious persons."

"Who says we're suspicious?" she demanded. "It's all in your suspicious head," and I cringed inwardly, waiting for the angry command to get out of the car.

He kept quiet though while he studied her face, his eyes narrowed, pale with reflected light. But she stared back at him, her jaw set and angry as if she were insulted, and his eyes gradually widened to a normal size, his tight mouth opened a little, as if it were relaxing, and he turned off his flashlight, then straightened up to his full height, handed me my cards and Carole's passport, and said, "You're strangers in the neighborhood, you understand. This is just a routine stop. Be careful on the freeway," and walked back to his car after I thanked him and started to put my cards away.

"He could have hassled us some more," I said, kicking the motor over, putting the car in gear, driving carefully onto the freeway, gradually building up my speed, glancing through the side window to see where he was, and searching in the side view mirror after I got on the freeway to see if he had followed us, added, "He was mean enough to do it."

"On what charge?" Carole asked, flipping her skirt up to get Sam's money out of her tights. "I don't believe it."

"Investigation," I said. "And you better believe it. They could keep us three days on it, too, long enough to check with the San Francisco police and find out that we're wanted there for punching cops in the mouth and selling acid no less. And back we'd go to hit the headlines and do some time."

The idea of appearing in the papers must have shocked her a little, because she didn't come back with a quick answer but sat there, facing forward, still holding onto the hem of her skirt with one hand and Sam's money with the other, and I was going to let it go at that, but Sam reached over her shoulder for his money and said, "Man, even if we had been busted, it wouldn't have been all that bad."

"What do you mean by that?" I asked, looking for his face in the mirror, angry already because he had been the most chickenshit one when the cop came around.

"All this evil you're so worried about. It'll pass, man," he said, leaning back, sticking his money in a jacket pocket, and stretching his legs out over the seat, his knees touching the ceiling. "We've got lives to go yet. There's even an absolute transcendence ahead of us when we're done with them. We're divine, man. We'll live through it."

"Man," I said and shook my head with the calculated intention of letting him know how simple I thought he was. "Man, that's an absolute sentimentalism."

"What do *you* mean?" Carole asked, as if I had attacked her.

"I mean that any kind of faith in a future life is just a cop-out on this one. Sam's picked up on a mongrelized form of Zen Buddhism but is coming on with the same kind of sentimentality that a Christian housewife has, meaning *she'll* get saved and *he* gets another chance to have fun, doesn't have to do anything to take care of himself in this life since he's still got others to use up. And while he's not sweating it, all the fascists are grabbing control of everything around, because no matter what they claim about a future life, they make the most of this one."

She didn't like that. Her face got sharp, seemed to draw toward the peak of her sharp nose, but didn't have an answer to fight back with, and though I didn't want to hurt her, Sam sat up as if he was going to argue, and piqued by him, I turned around and pointed at him, saying, "And you, man . . . . , judging by the way you just performed, you need another chance," scaring him, I guess, because his cheeks quivered. But my upper lip stayed taut against

52

my teeth, an ugly habit that I hated, and I said, "And I'll tell you something else, daddy. We're in this together now, and what you *don't* do might cost me my freedom. So what you *do* is my business and I'm going to make sure you do right."

My voice rang I was so hot. But Sam just sat there perfectly motionless, bunched up in the cramped space, his hands on his knees, his lips barely parted in a wry smile, as if he was afraid to really grin or argue for fear I'd get mad.

It was quiet in the car for a long time. But I was afraid to look at Carole and even avoided her eyes when I turned back to watch the road, sat there staring straight ahead, listening to the motor drone, sorry I'd gotten mad again, but not sorry enough to apologize. I then built the speed up to seventy-five just to occupy myself and tried to concentrate on my driving but the atmosphere was so charged, I got the feeling that Sam was touching Carole's arm again, and I jerked my head around to catch them at it.

But Carole was looking at me with her chin tucked in, her head down, and such a narrow-eyed expression of disgust on her face, that I blushed and suddenly asked, without thinking of it first: "What do you say we stop and buy some booze and get off this bummer trip if we can?"

She stared at me for a moment, then answered, finally, clearly, and very coldly: "Alright."

4

AFTER I PULLED OFF THE HIGHWAY—
the six lane freeway had ended below San Jose—and
stopped at a liquor store in Gilroy, I wanted to take
advantage of the chance she gave me to make up with
her by consenting to get some booze and didn't want
her to stay in the car with Sam when she was feeling
sorry for him and down on me, and I asked her to
come inside with me.

She gave me a quick but deep stare from semi-
profile, her far eye barely seen by me beyond the
bump in her nose, as if she had heard the care in my
voice. But then she must have seen it in my eyes
too, which was a lot considering how callous she
thought I was for laying it on Sam like I had, because she suddenly turned full face toward me and
examined my face in the light from the liquor store
as if I couldn't see her. She seemed to look at every
part of it, concentrating on one feature at a time, her
own face, in shadow, gradually losing its sharpness,
her eyes growing wider and softer, then suddenly
slanting down at the corners, almost closing, her
narrowed lashes darkening them, and she smiled
slightly, reached out and touched my chin and said,

"O.K.," as if she really did want to go with me and turned around and reached for her door handle.

But I was out my door and around to hers, holding it open for her before she could get out, hopping to it like a fool getting close to some twat and afraid he might lose it, and I could have come though I only smiled back when she gave me a quick smile for opening it and stepped across the sidewalk, but I beat her to the liquor store door and held that open for her too, followed her inside and asked her to pick what she wanted.

"Wine," she said in a disinterested way, then smiled as if my face had shown my disappointment and she wanted to make me feel better, but looked around for the wine racks just as quickly and walked off toward them, smiled politely too at the middle-aged storekeeper as she passed him and surprised him so much that his eyebrows rippled up into his forehead, and stayed that way until he noticed that I was looking at him. He then forced himself to look down, straightened the scratch pad next to the cash register, and stared at that until I passed him, and he thought I couldn't see him anymore, then looked up again.

But I did see him in the tall glass doors of the beer refrigerator, and he stared at Carole like he hadn't seen anything that good in his whole life—a broad six feet tall and beautiful too—or at least since he was young and couldn't remember anymore, now that he had trouble getting a hard-on. But I lost sight of him anyway when I opened the door to get myself a sixpack of Pabst Blue Ribbon, and he played it cool when I turned around and brought the sixpack back to the counter, pretended he was figuring out something on the scratch pad, though he looked up fast enough when Carole put the half-gallon jug of Red Mountain burgundy on the counter, slid it toward him, and smiled, very politely, again.

The old guy dared to smile back too, with his most being-polite-to-customers smile, his false teeth showing between his pale lips, until I slid the sixpack next to the jug and put my hand in my pocket for some money. Then he was very serious as he rang up the sale, gave me my change, put the jug and the sixpack in separate bags, but left the sixpack sitting on the counter and slid the jug in its sack to her, with another of his pale-lipped smiles, light glinting lewdly off his glasses. I thanked him without showing how amused I was, picked up my package, and followed Carole out the door, heard its bell tinkle for the last time behind me, and got into my MG, wondering whether I was going to get polite smiles all the way to TJ.

Sam's head lifted straight up when we got back into the car with the booze, his deep-set eyes shining, like the guy had forgotten all about the uptight scene we just had, and I couldn't help but like him and even feel sorry for him too, cramped the way he was back there: his hiking boots propped up on one of the sleeping bags between the seats, sticking up by a window, his knees touching the ceiling, his resting head jammed into the fastback window, and I asked, "Whata' ya have, man? Beer or wine?"

He leaned over and took Carole's jug for an answer, smiled at me when he swayed back to his semiprone position, pulled the jug out of the bag, and twisted the cap loose. He had to turn his head to the side though, to drink out of the full jug without spilling it, under the low ceiling, and he drank down several mouthfuls before he handed it back to her, his mouth still full and his cheeks puffed.

"We'll all be grooving pretty quick, if that keeps up," I said to him, trying to be friendly, and he nodded his head while he swallowed. I cracked a can of beer myself, pulled off the snap-top ring, dropped it in the bag, and after a deep swallow, started the car and pulled back onto the highway, made sure I didn't drive too fast in town too, since the highway wouldn't turn into a freeway again until we got to Gonzales, which was another small town about fifty miles away, and I cruised at twenty-five miles per-hour past a business section that consisted mostly of darkened storefronts and deserted streets, with only a few neon signs burning, even on a Saturday night.

Carole only took a single swallow after she got the jug though, barely wet her lips it looked like to me, and gave me a dutiful quirk of her mouth for a smile when she lowered the jug, then handed it back to Sam without taking any more, and Sam looked at me and grinned, then chug-a-lugged it again, while I knocked off my first can without bringing it down from my mouth, liking the first swallows the best anyway, but wanting to get busted in the skull right away so I wouldn't be so uptight all the time, would quit picking on Sam, and then wouldn't have to worry over what Carole thought of my hardness, or Sam playing sympathy fingertap with her either.

I watched her when I was drinking it down, hoping she'd look at me, but she was gazing ahead at the highway, and when I finished the beer and bent the can in half with my thumbs, while steering the car with my forearms, then asked her to drop it back in the sack and get me another one, she gave me an unopened one without looking at me, and I said, "Smile, Carole," and got her to grin at least, though I had to open the beer can myself, which wasn't much, but was inconsiderate of her whether she did it on purpose or not.

Still, she was trying to be nice in a sulking kind of way, and took another dutiful sip when Sam handed the jug back to her, and since she was only drinking because I had asked her to, I tried not to worry about her lack of enthusiasm and kept myself busy driving and drinking, finished a second beer and a third, and was working on a fourth by the time we got to Salinas, where I asked Sam how much he had left. He held the half-full jug up for me to see but couldn't hold it steady and it swayed back and forth in front of his fuzzy eyes, which looked so smashed, Carole and I both started laughing, and that broke the distance between us and she touched my arm in a warm, casual manner to share her glee with me.

"Give her some," I said and she took the jug and filled her mouth for the first time, then genuinely smiled at me after she had swallowed, which warmed me up so much I started telling them about this Mexican cat I had met on the beach at Ensenada once who drank pints of straight wood alcohol— Twin Pines, I think it was called—and who claimed he could get me a pound of grass for fifteen dollars.

His brown eyes were so diluted by juice that they were encircled by pale moons and the whites were a cloudy yellow. "Eee-wo Gee-ma! Eee-wo Gee-ma!" he kept saying, claiming that he'd fought with the American army there in World War Two, as proof of his loyalty to me, and that he'd return with the pound of grass even though I gave him the money first. But when I gave him fifty cents and told him to come back with some beer for both of us, I never saw him again.

Carole drank and giggled throughout the story and Sam broke up every time I added some detail about how the guy was dressed in raggedy clothes, no socks on, an overcoat, five sizes too big for him, on a hot day, and about a ten-day beard, and carried away by the friendly atmosphere and feeling that I could speak frankly and now heal the rift I had caused between us earlier, I said, "That's why I get so uptight, you guys, over not being careful all the time. I've been almost burned and busted so many times, in Mexico too, that I know what to expect and what you've got to do to keep it from happening."

They both stared at me for a moment, then glanced at each other and were totally quiet. All I could hear was the car motor hum until Sam leaned back in his seat and shifted around to settle himself into a comfortable semiprone position once more, his head resting on Carole's knapsack in the fastback window, his long body slumping down, settling into every low spot like a blanket, his knees touching the ceiling, the jug resting on his belly, and his eyes closing like he wanted to get some sleep.

WHAT NOW MY LOVE

Carole slumped down in the front seat, staring out the window for a while, then closed her eyes too, and I let the whole thing drop, having pulled my too-frank fuckup for the day, embarrassed people by being too outspoken as usual, and by being a little insincere too, because I *had* been trying to clean up for myself after all. I drove for a long time with no other sound in the car but the drone of the motor, my mind stewing with the whole scene, meaning: how was I going to make sure that I didn't get busted and yet keep her love too. Because if they didn't take precautions, I had to and I would, even if it hurt me with her. I was determined to stay free though it cost me comfort, happiness, and even her love.

Sam started breathing heavily, came very close to snoring when we were passing through Paso Robles, and I glanced back at him with his noise and noticed how her breast and stomach rose and fell in the dim light of the dashboard, then studied her face as she lay with her head resting on the back of her seat, her chin up, the strong cleft in it accentuating the delicacy of its tip. Yet it somehow seemed crooked, as if her jaw didn't fit well against her upper teeth, which caused her lips to look pursed most of the time, until she got hot, that is, when she'd coo through a little air pocket in the center, or angry, when she'd twist them into ugly shapes. But her coloring, the pale, icy blond of her hair and her very pale blue eyes, her pale skin, which was touched by rose spots on the cheekbones, and her long, slender body, made her very beautiful in spite of the irregularity of her mouth, the bump on her narrow nose, the way her eyes drooped slightly down at the corners. I watched her sleep, grooving on her beauty, for the whole four hours it took me to drive to the shoreline at Santa Barbara, and I hoped she'd stay asleep until we passed through Los Angeles so there wouldn't be another hassle over picking up some joints in Venice, compounding this bring-down.

The sea looked mighty dark on my right, out past the beach houses, which seemed to stretch in a long, unbroken silhouette all the way to San Diego, and the eastern sky was still a gloomy purple on my left, like the sun was still an hour or so away from coming up yet, though it was almost six in the morning by my guess, based on the 334 miles we had traveled from San Francisco. Up ahead of me the sky was overcast, not just dark—as if morning fog covered the coast all the way to TJ, where if things didn't warm up between me and Carole quick, I'd end up on my own and fast.

She sighed in her sleep then and leaned against the door, her head against the window, then sighed again and twisted completely around on the seat so that she was facing me, though still leaning against the door, the side of her head against the seat back, strands of her hair hanging over it, looking gorgeous, the two main strands sweeping down from the part in the middle of her head and cupping her lowered face in pale shadow, the silver strands parted at the bottom by the cleft of her chin, which made a faint ring of light above her breasts and made me want to kiss her.

She sighed and shifted again, stretched out toward me more and lifted her bent legs up on the seat, but one slipped down, making me fear she'd wake up, and swung open, and I could see the soft mound of her snatch between her spread thighs, and I wanted to touch it but didn't want to wake her, then touched it anyway, lightly, cupping my right hand over it from above, letting the heel of my hand rest in the hollow of her cunt, pressing softly on the springy patch of pubic hairs under the tights.

She could feel it in her sleep and the tendons in her loins tightened as she pushed her box slightly forward, then relaxed like she had drifted off in her sleep again. But my dick got hard immediately and I pressed harder, pushed the heel of my hand deeper into the suck of her soft hole, and she spread her legs even wider and pushed back again, pumped a couple of times, then rolled her head a little away from the back of the seat, opened her eyes and looked at me.

We continued to stare at each other—me barely watching the dark road out of an eye corner, her eyes slanting down at the corners like a cat about to purr, as I pumped with my whole arm, rocked the heel of my hand into the soft hollow in the middle of her, easily, but firmly, and finally made her purse her lips, make a tiny air pocket in the center of them, blow out her breath in a low, cooing moan, swing her head back and forth as if in ecstasy, and pump to meet me.

I got hotter and pressed harder, forcing the heel of my hand as deep as it would go within her, and her eyelids fluttered and sank down, completely hiding her eyes, her lips spreading in just the hint of a smile, using my shove to work against, rolling her body around on my hand, arching her back, her ass rising up off the seat so high that my hand slipped off, cupped as it was from above, and I had to grab the wheel with both hands to keep the car from veering off the road, though there wasn't another car on it at this late hour between night and morning.

"Pull them off," I whispered, waving my hand down, so Sam, who was breathing heavily in the back seat, wouldn't hear.

She nodded and smiled in agreement, the cleft in her chin so handsome that I wanted to kiss it. But my dick was hard and I wanted some of her pussy first and didn't kiss her at all. And she braced her back and shoulders up against the door, lifted her hips off the seat, flipped her skirt up to her waist, and slipped her tights down past her belly, the slash of her navel, the dark mound of her snatch. The two lip-folds of her cunt were so close to my face for the second she took to pull the tights as far down as her knees that my dick twitched and discharged a little and I could feel the sticky wet on the inside of my thigh.

She kissed me though when she got them off, leaned over the gear box and stuck her tongue in my mouth, then kissed my neck, and put her hand down on my dick to stroke it. I stuck my finger in her pussy too and started pumping with it, faster and harder, until her moans turned to soft grunts, "Uh-uh-uh," and she rolled back to the door, her head against the window, and spread her legs, braced them, one on the floor, the other on the seat, its knee almost touching the ceiling, and pumped to meet me, showing me the whole underside of her body, from the crack between her legs to the rounds of her ass, and kept snapping her hips that way, meeting my pumping finger, slapping against it.

I got so hung up watching my finger go in and out, seeing her taut body snap, snap, snap, grunts come out of her pouting lips and her slanted lids flutter at me that my car drifted across the lanes to the shoulder and I had to jerk the wheel hard to keep on the road.

She looked up to see if we were O.K., then smiled and moaned again when, with my finger still going in her, I gradually slowed down, pulled off the pavement onto the shoulder and came to a stop without jerking the car. I then left the motor running to give a covering noise and convince Sam in his sleep that he was still being driven down the highway, since I wasn't about to share my broad with him, like a lot of acid heads do, and didn't even dig the *idea* of *any*body watching me ball my chick, especially a cat who might have fucked her before.

But she was really hot and leaned over, still cooing, and started running her fingers through my hair before I could get myself turned around in my seat to finger her better. But I kept fingering her and pumped it into her with much more snap because of my better position, no driving to worry about, and she started thrashing her head around, whipping her long hair about, and cooing and moaning and raising her snatch up so high she seemed about to come, though I knew she never had in her life—with me or any other guy.

But that pussy looked so good to me that I pulled my finger out and rammed my face right into it, kissed the moist lips hard and jammed my tongue as deep as it would go within her. She moaned then and dug her fingernails into my scalp and pressed my whole head hard against her so that her soft pubic hairs were against my nose, my cheeks, my nostrils full of her clean, natural odor, my face up so high with her back arched like it was that if Sam had looked he could have seen me. But she couldn't keep it arched and dropped down to the seat again and spread her legs so wide it looked like she was going to do the splits, her right leg reaching over the steering wheel and her left leg balanced along the top of my seat's backrest.

I turned over on my stomach, then, cupped my hands under the cheeks of her ass, stuck my legs into the space under the dashboard, let them find their own room among the pedals, then started pumping my dick against the seat edge and flipping the tip of my tongue back and forth against the pelvic bone at the top of her cunt, and she snapped and cooed and moaned and thrashed her head around and I didn't even give a fuck if Sam heard, it got so good.

But then she pinched her thighs so tightly around my head that I had trouble breathing *and* hearing. There was a roar in my ears like a strong wind, but her moans still kept getting louder and louder, and I got worried again that Sam might hear and even tried to see him out of the corner of my eye, but couldn't see anything but the inside of her thighs.

Yet the idea that he might hear made me want to get it over with, and I started pumping faster as I ate her. My body started arching off the seat, balanced on my dick. My bent legs lifted off the floor.

WHAT NOW MY LOVE

My skin got wet with sweat under my turtle neck. But hungup on her cunt, I wanted to kiss it and lick it and swallow it and pump my tongue into it all at the same time.

And I got hotter and hotter and my body arched stiffer and stiffer as a beautiful thrill began in my buttocks, seemed to draw juice from as far down as my cramped toes and rise up with my tightened thighs, but, simultaneously, come down from as high up as the tingling numbness of my scalp too, trickle down my backbone, tighten with my stomach, bunch up in my groin, surge forward with it and suddenly explode with pulsing waves of come out my throbbing dick.

My whole body froze rigid with the final spasm for an exalted second or two or three, a dragged out fourth, my tongue kept going slower and slower, my pumping softer and softer, her snapping lighter and lighter, her moans shorter and shorter, until we finally stopped together, and I opened my mouth wide and sucked her cunt lips into mine for a final kiss, then let go and collapsed, my face on her stomach, my body a dead weight across the gearshift box and my seat, my knees resting on the floor, my feet crossed above the pedals.

Her ass sagged down into my cupped hands then and she opened her thighs and looked gently down on me, ran her fingers through my hair and cooed a little, then bent over, lifted up my head by the chin, lingered for a moment with her face close to mine, whispered, "I love you," and stuck her tongue deep into my mouth.

5

MY HANDS STARTED SWEATING WHEN
we drove around the curve of the highway from San
Diego some time after noon and I saw the long row
of yellow carports, with American customs agents in
brown uniforms inspecting cars crossing over the
border into the U.S., and the single one-room guard-
house at one end of the carports, where the Mexican
customs agents usually sat in the shade and waved
the American cars past with a minimum of questions, but who might, in our case, stop us and turn
us over to the American police, and I wiped my
hands on my cords because they were making the
steering wheel slippery.

I was sweating some too because though it was
still a little overcast with ocean clouds in the early
afternoon—the film of clouds so thin you could see
the blue through it—the sky looked marbled and the
hot sun burned through the windshield, making me
wish I had something on other than my heavy green
turtle neck, which kept all my body heat in.

Carole seemed to feel my mood, and though she
looked clean and neat and was dressed perfectly for
the warm weather in her green chiffon minidress,
there was a faint outline of pink on her lid rims and

dissipation shadows under her eyes, the only sign of two nights in a row without much sleep, perhaps five or six hours at most, which gave her a vaguely disturbed look.

And though I was a little red-eyed and floating from no sleep at all and the last two cans of beer, which I had knocked off after eating her, Sam, who had been sipping on the jug since he woke up a little while after Carole and I had finished balling, looked remarkably good for all the juice he had had—the jug was only a quarter full now, and his small eyes which were naturally deep-set and shadowed most of the time, had a couple of red streaks through them but were steady and alert and his tan skin glowed like he had just got out of the hot sun, not barely slept. He was so unconcerned about crossing the border in fact, that he leaned his head down by the back of my seat, turned it sideward, tilted up the bottle and took a long swallow.

"Down with it, man. Those American border guards could bust us for drinking in a car," I said, noticing the blue stains on his fingers, and Carole looked at me with a quizzical frown which was a real bring-down after a whole morning of caresses and smiles from her, and I was doubly unhappy when I slowed and then stopped in the shade of the carport and looked nervously about for plainclothes narcotics inspectors, though I knew that the odds that they might be waiting at the border for us were far out.

"How far down are you going?" the Mexican guard asked, after he had got off the stool in the doorway, but I had been searching his face for signs of recognition of me and was so unprepared to answer, that I worked my jaw a couple of times with my mouth open before I finally said, "Mazatlán," and could have kicked myself in the ass for telling him exactly where we were headed.

But he just pointed to a low, trailer-size wooden shack with a set of steps at each end to enter and leave by about a block ahead of us and said, "Get your visas over there," and waved us by.

"Maybe we shouldn't get our visas here at all," I said creeping in second gear toward the shack, knowing I could ruin the good thing that Carole and I had going, and which I hoped would last until Mazatlán, where we could relax, live alone without Sam, and probably could get along together when there wasn't so much pressure on us.

"Why not?" she asked, frowning again and sitting up straight in her bucket seat, her head nearly touching the ceiling.

"Because they can trace us if they decide to, and they might even question that border guard and get him to remember what I said, then start looking for us in Mazatlán."

"Oh, come on, Miles," Carole said and shook her head. "For all the San Francisco police know, we're hiding out in the Haight-Ashbury. They're not going to check down here."

"They might," I insisted as I pulled up by the shack and stopped. "What if somebody got hurt with those guns we heard or maybe even killed? They'd come right across the border to get us." When she shook her head again, I said, "Besides, we don't have smallpox certificates, and they'll insist that we get shots in town before they'll give us a visa."

"So you and Sam will get shots," she said. "We'd have to do the same thing someplace else, no matter where we got the visas. Dig? And that would be a drag. Why don't we get the whole thing over with?"

"If we get them someplace else," I said, turning in my seat so I could see him as well as her, "beside the most obvious place, say Mexicali, we can throw them off the track. Just a little safety-first might make all the difference in our lives."

"Ah, Miles, don't be so paranoid *all* the time," Carole said and shook her head like she felt sorry for me, making me feel like an old man though I was only twenty-eight, and I couldn't think of an answer before Sam said:

"We don't have to sweat it that much, Miles. The fuzz is going to look all over the Haight-Ashbury for me first, and even if they did check the border afterwards, we'd be long gone and lost from sight in Mexico."

"Let's not sweat it then," Carole said, opening her door and taking advantage of my hesitation. "Let's get the visas and get it over with. Don't bring us down any more."

Sam pushed the back of her seat down to get out too and forced me into getting out myself, though I knew I shouldn't do it, just like I knew that hippie in the bright silk shirt was a cop, because of the uneasy feeling in my belly, and the quivery feeling stayed with me and even grew as we got closer to the shack, and I stopped them on the dirt path before either of them could go in and said, "You know, we really ought to buy a paper and see if we can find out what happened in the Haight last night, so we could know how serious it is or isn't. We ought to at least find out where we stand, and then go on from there, make our plans on the most information possible."

Both of them were annoyed by my insistence. Sam had a smug expression on his face, a near smile on his mouth, and slouched as if he were bored. Carole said, "We're only two feet away from getting our visas, and I'd rather get them now and take any kind of chance we've got to take rather than have you torture us over all the terrible things that might happen to us when we do get them for another hot day on the way to Mexicali or where ever you want to go, and until we're so damn paranoid and brought down we'd have been better off to get caught!" then turned and stepped up into the building, and with a shrug of his shoulders and a weak smile, Sam stepped up into the shack after her, and I followed him in.

There was only one other tourist in the shack at the time, a middle-aged, sunburned American in a flowery, short-sleeved sportshirt, who watched Carole as one Mexican cop typed up his visa for him and the other took Carole's passport from her and didn't take more than five minutes to make out her visa, which is very fast in Mexico. And except for a few quick glances of his dark brown eyes at her tall body, her long legs in those pale green tights, and her blond hair that Mexican cats just about come in their pants in the street over, his mouth was very tight under his thin mustache, and he pointed to the line on the visa for her signature and took her money without saying a single word.

WHAT NOW MY LOVE

He did O.K. with me too until he got to the smallpox vaccination certificate, then looked up at me
from under one of his heavy Indian lids and shook
his head and pointed a plump finger at the application line where the smallpox date was supposed to
be filled in, and started to hand me back my application, his tight mouth shaped to say no, when,
already prepared for this, I leaned down and showed
him my birth certificate again, with a five-dollar bill
under it, and he pinched the certificate tightly between his fat fingers and examined the birth date
very closely, then nodded his head and spun around
on his swivel chair to the typewriter and finished
typing up my visa.

Since he knew that all three of us were together, I
took it for granted that he'd be ready to deal quickly
with Sam too, and after I paid my fee, I put my
hand in my pocket and pulled out another five-dollar
bill, then held it cupped in my hand next to my
thigh and waited for the right chance to give it to
him, feeling awkward about it though and afraid to
say anything about it in advance since Sam didn't
see me pay the guy off, and I didn't want to tell
him about it in an obvious way. But when the guy
got to the smallpox date, saw that it wasn't filled in,
said, "You got to have a smallpox shot first," and
started to give the application back to Sam and I
started to hand him the five-dollar bill, Sam said in
a loud voice:

"You just let him have one without a shot!"

"Whot?" the bull said, his cheeks turning red,
glancing over at his partner, who looked up, and
ashamed because his partner knew he didn't get his

mordida, which is bribery and part of a man's income in the Mexican civil service, in a dignified way, he said, "Get out!" and pointed at the door.

"Hell no! Why should I?" Sam said, and Carole stepped next to the desk and said:

"Public servants don't have any right to order people around. You just do your job," and the surprised cop sat back so far in his swivel chair that it banged against the wall, where he stayed for a moment, staring up at her, and afraid he was going to bust Sam right then, I said:

"*'Spensa me,*" meaning excuse me in Spanish, speaking the guy's language to make him feel good, though he probably already knew I was a spic by my last name. *"Es posible a leer* this?" I pointed to the small print on Sam's draft card with my index finger and the tip of the five-dollar bill, the number five showing and the rest of the bill crushed in my palm, hoping he wasn't too mad to go for it.

He sat back up when he saw the tip of the five and, sliding his chair close to the desk again, paid careful attention to where I was pointing, then said, *"Sí,"* and pinched the tip of the card and the bill between his fingers and even started to pull them out of my hand when Sam said, "What's that got to do with it?" and he let go and squeaked back in his chair, his cheeks darkening all over again.

"Shut up, Sam!" I said and stared at him hard, and he kept quiet. Carole was quiet too.

"*'Spensa me por mis amigos,*" I said and bowed a little, then pointed again to the draft card with the tip of the bill and the cop squeaked back to his desk and paid polite attention to me, glanced at Sam once more, who didn't look back, then pinched the tip of the bill to the draft card again, took both out of my hand, put the bill under some papers, then typed up Sam's visa, while I gave Sam the hard eye to make sure that he didn't wise-off again.

"*Gracias*," I said when the guy had finished and handed Sam his visa, and I kicked Sam's shoe to make him do the same, but he just ignored me, paid the fee, signed the visa, and walked away without a word.

"*Gracias*," I said again for him and followed him and Carole out the door.

"Why'd you bribe him? I wouldn't have given him a penny," Sam said after we'd walked out of hearing range on the dirt path, glancing at Carole after he spoke as if expecting her to support him.

"To keep us all from getting busted, asshole!" I said and was mad enough at him for risking a bust to blast him in the mouth if he pushed it far enough.

He looked at Carole again, but she merely glanced at each of us and kept walking, and though he looked at her two or three more times on the way back to the car as if still expecting her to take his side, when she didn't, he got into the back seat without another word and even smiled when she said, "Let's not argue. Let's go cop and have some fun now."

"O.K.," I said, though I wasn't so hot to go have some fun and still had misgivings over crossing the border at such an easily traceable place, but I didn't want to hassle with Sam and did want to score and told her: "We can probably make it from a cabstand near the jai-alai games."

WHAT NOW MY LOVE

She smiled and so did Sam, and I drove past a mile of dust-gray wooden shacks and weed fields, an old wooden viaduct, into the west end of the business section of TJ, which had adobe huts, with only black holes in them for the windows and doors, all over the brown hills around it. But the main drag was so crowded with cars, thousands of them, counting the parked ones, and there were so many thousands of people on foot, mostly Americans, who had come across for some Sunday fun, and, I guessed, a bullfight, swarming over the two-foot-high sidewalks that I started to cross it, intending to take a parallel street on the other side, which I hoped would miss most of the traffic, but Carole said, "Go down the main street, Miles, so we can dig everything." And when I did, she put her dark glasses on, which were so big they slid down to the bump in her nose, leaned forward to get a better view through the windshield, and said, "Wow! It's like a carnival!"

The sun reflected in bright, eye-watering pools from the metallic roofs and chrome bumpers and grills and glass windows of thousands and thousands of American cars, shimmered in heat waves that blurred the pastel shades of the one-story buildings, distorted the shapes of people, gave the bright colors of all the goods for sale, the glazed ceramic dishes, the rugs, the flowers, the serapes, the sombreros, a wavering, fluid heat, and made me wish I had my dark glasses on.

Vendors with trays of cheap jewelry and rings all over their fingers walked up and down the high sidewalks, hustling their wares. Doormen, stationed in front of stores, tried to talk the tourists into going inside by calling out in broken English the great souvenirs they had for sale. Food carts, painted bright red and green and orange and blue, were parked on every corner, their dark-complexioned owners in washed out work clothes, selling tacos and enchiladas and refried beans, whose spicy smells floated in through our open windows.

Carole broke out laughing when we saw a red-faced Southerner, now transplanted to the aircraft plants of Southern California, sitting with his skinny wife and two kids in a donkey cart with huge sombreros on their heads, behind two zebra-striped jackasses, having their picture taken by a Mexican who had his head hidden under the black hood of an old-fashioned tripod camera, then started beating out a bongo rhythm on her knees when we passed a cabaret with its doors wide open and the bouncy latin sounds of the combo inside came floating out to us in the middle of the street. So I started thumping out a conga base-beat on the steering wheel with the heels of my hands, made a deep, resonant sound that backed up her pitter-patter and was joined by Sam, who came a rappatapping in too on the back of Carole's seat with some counterpoint.

We got so carried away that we kept up the beat, sometimes varying it a little, but smiling all the time, all the way through town to where the traffic finally thinned near the block-sized yellow jai-alai games building, which was just across the street from the cabstand I wanted to score from, though the stand was around the corner and off the main drag, which I liked, and Carole and Sam both stopped drumming when I did to turn the wheel; then all of us quiet and serious again, went around the corner and moved slowly by the stand, while I scanned the whole corner looking for the guy, but only saw one dark-complexioned dude, who was the wrong man, sitting in his cab.

"Not here," I said.

"Hit on this guy for him, then," Carole said and I parked my MG diagonally to the curb a few car spaces from the cab and went over to hit on the guy.

But the cabbie started wagging his head from side to side, his full Indian lips sullen and dark, as soon as I tried to describe the little guy I was looking for in my piecemeal Spanish, which was functional enough but sure wasn't fluent. My family had immigrated to the U.S. from Spain too many generations before and intermarried with too many other national types for Spanish to be a second language. The guy just wagged his head and stared down at his shoe on the brake pedal, its toe leather looking like perforated cardboard fashioned in a wing tip design, white showing through on the curling edges. And except for a quick glance at Carole through his stiff-lashed lids when she got out of the car and came over to find out what was wrong, followed by Sam, he kept staring at his shoe, and I was staring at it too when Carole said, "Hit on him for some speed then, Miles."

"*Sabe donde hay speed?*" I asked, without thinking about it, spoiled by a long habit of scoring easily from that corner, of having to turn down Spanish fly and junk just about every time I came around because I didn't use anything but weed.

"Whot?" the cabbie said, turning his round face

on me, glaring at me with his black eyes. "You ask me for that?"

"Why not?" Carole said, almost grinning, and I leaned away from the cab to get out of his striking range, then stepped up on the curb and said, "Let's go," not about to mess with the guy any more. Both of them followed me, thankfully—Sam with an embarrassed grin—but Carole said, "Why not leave the car there and walk down the main drag until we find somebody?"

"With this guy mad enough at us to turn us in?" I said, moving toward my car. "I'm not about to leave my MG around here so he can hip the heat to us and have them waiting for us when we get back. Let's go."

They got back in the car without any complaints and I drove it around the block, looking for a parking spot, but had to go almost completely around it and almost to the corner where the cabstand was and even then had to U-turn into a spot on the opposite side of the main street in order to get one.

"It's only around the corner from the guy, but it's out of his sight and we could have gone back across the border as far as he's concerned," I said and, ignoring the pitying glance that Carole gave me and shared with Sam over my paranoia, got out of the car and up on the high curb, where the fiesta colors of the street stretched out in front of me made me feel pretty good, though I knew the beers bubbling in my brain had something to do with it. Yet, we had gotten across the border without being stopped or hassled in any kind of way, which meant that we weren't being tailed or traced so far and

were relatively cool in Mexico, and I wanted to turn
on to some mellow pot and get back in the groove
with Carole.

So down the street we went to score if we could,
all three of us already loaded some off the booze and
no sleep—Carole had had a few slugs of that wine
during the last lap of the trip to the border too. We
started having fun when we passed the first plump
pitchman in front of the first cabaret, who stepped in
front of us in his double-breasted suitcoat and full-
pleated, unmatched slacks, his whole outfit more
suitable to the late forties than the late sixties, and
said, "Come on in, boys, and deeg thees hur gurls,"
and smiled when we busted up laughing. We grinned
everytime we passed one of the guys, who was gener-
ally short, plump and brown-skinned, with coarse
black or graying hair, and who fractured his American slang with his Mexican accent just like the first
guy did. I noticed too that the pitchmen would hit
on everybody who passed them, including the girls
in capri's and short miniskirts, everybody except the
bikers. They all seemed to hang out at one bar, where
no one else but they went in and which didn't have a
pitchman out in front, and which I avoided so as not
to get into a fight—since they took it for granted that
we, hippies, that is, wouldn't fight back. Though I
was prepared to bust any one of them in the mouth
if they messed with me or my chick and then run like
hell to keep from getting my brains kicked in by the
rest of them, they made me feel a little unhappy anyway because they reminded me of Hutch back in the
Haight-Ashbury and all that we were running from.

We kept on having fun anyway though, digging

all the bongo drums, rugs, sandals, clay figurines and wood-carved Don Quixotes, all of them skinny and looking just alike, no matter what the size, as well as, for me anyway, the groovy American chicks in miniskirts who had come across the border dressed lightly for the hot day. About every fifty feet or so we had to refuse our way by some salesman with a jewelry tray hanging from his neck, rings covering his fingers, watches all over his wrists, who'd step in front of us and try to sell us some "genuine" gold and silver jewelry with true gems.

But we were still looking for dope and when we'd get close to a cabstand, which were always on corners, I'd separate from Carole and Sam, wait until they disappeared in the crowd a few feet away and would then hit on one of the cabbies, ask him if he knew where I could score. But each guy would either turn off and snub me or would answer no immediately, without any attempt to be polite. I got turned down for about a mile down the main drag, and, discouraged, not having fun anymore, crossed it to try my luck on the other side, wondering why things were so chilly when I saw a big, red truck cross an intersection a block away, with a speaker on top of its cab and a long, white banner attached to its side gates with NARCOTICA spelled out in red block letters and some announcement of a town meeting, and I finally woke up to what was wrong and how much things had changed in the town since the hippie thing went off big in America and every college kid in Southern California came across the border to score.

WHAT NOW MY LOVE

"Hey!" I said, after I caught up with Carole and Sam. "Did you see that red truck?"

Neither of them had and when I told them what I'd seen and that that was probably why I was having so much trouble, they both nodded, but wouldn't comment because they were afraid I'd use it as an excuse to stop looking, and tired of getting turned down, hot and dizzy from the long, slow walk, I suggested we stop in at a bar and have a beer, and they quickly agreed. But just as we were going into the place, I noticed some big Mexican cat in a blue, double-breasted suit burning us, and though I didn't know if it was because of Carole or because he just wanted to look at the hippies, I decided to hit on him, told Carole and Sam to wait for me inside and went over to the guy.

"Sure," he said. He was tall for a Mexican, young, and looked very heavy in the double-breasted suitcoat which he kept buttoned across his full belly, even in the heat. "Follow me."

Which I did, after I gave Carole and Sam a glance through the doorway of the club to let them know that something was happening, followed the guy across the main drag and down a side street, staying about twenty feet behind him, watching the hurried way he walked, swung his arms far back and made his coat billow, his slacks ripple, and wondered if anybody might guess that I was with him, might notice the similarity of our directions among the other people on the sidewalk, but didn't worry about it either and followed him for four or five blocks to a pottery yard with about fifteen or twenty tourists in it, where he gave me a sign to wait and went on around the corner.

The yard was full of beautifully glazed dishes of every type: bowls and plates and platters and vases and tea cups and pitchers, mainly of a blue color, with different variations, some almost purple, others aquamarine, but all streaked with deep reds and greens, bright oranges and yellows, which melted and ran down the blue backgrounds like candle wax, and for a moment I wished that I was on acid, which I had only taken once in my life, so that I could really appreciate the flowing colors. I then thought of how surprised I'd been when I first turned on and saw the world shift and waver and boil and burn like a Van Gogh painting. I had marveled then at how turned on he must have been all the time but understood, too, how he couldn't stand it either and killed himself.

The beer was doing its share to my head too, though, and I leaned against a fence post and let my brain idle like a car motor, going nowhere, doing nothing, but running just the same, while I grooved on all the beautiful colors and enjoyed the crisp smell of the hay that the dishes were packed in and which was scattered all over the yard, as well as the salesmen who all seemed to argue with the customers. I got some fun too out of breaking the law in the middle of all the unsuspecting people— a feeling I had enjoyed every so often before the misery I had endured on the long run from the heat took that infrequent pleasure away, a pleasure that Carole still enjoyed, and I was even a little sorry when the guy came back, gave me the hard eye from

one end of the fence, disappeared back around it, and
I had to leave my post and follow him.

We walked down another block to an old govern-
ment-owned gas station, which was so run down it
looked abandoned but had two attendants loitering
around inside the garage in the shade, whom I saw
when I followed the guy into the men's head, which
didn't have a door nor a handle to flush the brown-
crudded toilet bowl with. The whole place stank of
hot piss and the dealer seemed to be in a big hurry
to get out of it himself by the quick way he turned
around to face me as soon as I stepped inside, out of
sight of the street, and pulled a newspaper wrapped
like a cone out of his inside coat pocket, and said,
"Here."

"How much?" I asked, without lifting a hand
to take it.

"Fifteen dollars," he said, pushing it closer to my
chest, and frowning.

"Hell no," I said, "I can buy a whole pound for
thirty dollars down here and *that* much grass for five
bucks in San Francisco. I'll give you thirty dollars
for a pound and nothing less. I'm not going to pay
that kind of price."

He stood there staring at me with his arm out and
his dark forehead wrinkled, his mouth open, as if
he couldn't figure out why I didn't take the cone,
then he shoved it at me again, shook it twice to get
me to take it out of his hand, and said, "Fifteen dollars!" once more. Which surprised me. He was the
first Mexican I had ever seen who didn't bargain,
who didn't ask a higher price than he expected to
get, no matter what he was selling. But it was still

too much and I said, "Thirty dollars for a pound and that's all."

"Shit!" the guy said, his dark face turning purple with anger, and he stuffed the cone back in his pocket and strode out of the toilet, muttering, "Shit! Shit! Shit!"

I felt sort of unhappy as I watched him ruffle up the street, still muttering to himself, and I wondered if the cost of grass had gone up with the heat on it, he was so set on the single price and so nervous about making the sale, but I discounted that on the grounds that they charged a lot for a little and a little for a lot. Yet I was afraid I'd regret not buying from him and getting the score over with until we got down to Mazatlán, where Sam's buddies would probably have a lot of grass on them and would sell us some for a decent price. And that feeling bothered me all the way back to the club where I got brought down even further when I walked in and saw Carole and Sam sitting at the bar, sharing a third round of beer and some private joke they didn't bother to tell me about when I sat down by them.

"Did you?" Carole asked, finally recognizing me; the smile still on her lips from the joke.

"The guy wanted far too much money for a little bit."

"How much?" Sam asked, leaning familiarly against Carole, who was between us.

"Fifteen dollars for a big lid when thirty would get us a pound."

"Couldn't we bargain with him?" Carole asked, and when I told her that he split, salty, when I wouldn't pay his price, she said, "Shit!" just like the guy, which I didn't appreciate after the work and the worry I had put into the wasted deal.

Sam just shrugged his shoulders though, like the booze was good enough for him, and leaned away from Carole to drink some more of his beer, and she turned toward him and drank from her glass too, and ignored and worried that they might get juiced and hungup in the bar, I said, "We better get moving. Our side of the street's shadowed already. It must be three or four by now."

They shared a glance over their beer glasses on that but didn't comment and when Sam took another slow sip of his beer like he'd like to stay in the cool bar a while longer, I said, since I was uptight over trudging those hot streets while they relaxed inside in the shade: "Let's go score, you guys, or get the hell out of town."

They looked at each other again, but Carole did turn on her stool and start to get down, though she went so slowly to show her displeasure she could have been climbing down a ladder, not getting off a bar stool. Sam just shrugged his shoulders, knocked off his beer, and paid with an indifferent slowness as if to prove that nothing I did could ever bother him, and joined me and Carole out on the sidewalk. But outside, after we crossed the street to try the opposite side on the way back to the car, they started walking close to the buildings like I wasn't around, leaving me to walk on the outside of the sidewalk, separated from them most of the time by the flow of people moving the opposite way. They looked like beautiful lovers together too: tall, dark, and handsome Sam in a Prince Valiant haircut and white tunic, stepping long and lazy next to this six-foot queen with pale, yellow hair and a gauze-thin minidress who seemed to be a natural mate for him, which made me feel like an ugly midget on the outside, losing a couple of inches of height with the slope of the sidewalk, sweating from the long walk, my face powdered with dust, my throat dry even, and with my resentment against both of them about the only thing going for me. I got so brought down that I was considering stopping them and asking them if they wanted me around and, if not, to let me know, right then, so I could split, and I was also prepared to blast Sam in the mouth and to tell Carole to go fuck herself, if it went far enough.

Carole must have finally noticed me walking by myself because she glanced at me a couple of times when Sam was talking, and then slowed a little so I'd walk *with* them not behind them and even spaced herself so that she was more equally between us, though people had to pass on both sides of her and one sailor tried to rub up against her, forcing her to press up against me to avoid him, and she smiled after he passed.

But I was still brought down and didn't bother to hit on anybody for a couple of blocks, and when we started down a third block and passed a group of cabbies without my sounding them, Carole asked, "Why aren't you hitting on anybody, Miles?"

"What for?" I asked back, my top lip flat against my teeth, and she squinted like the sun was in her eyes though she was wearing her dark glasses, didn't answer, and muttered something to Sam, who looked at me, shrugged his shoulders, then nodded his head and dropped behind us when we passed a leather goods shop where he hit on a pitchman who had tried to get him to go inside the place.

We were a couple of stores down when he did, but the rank smell of the leather was still perceptible, and I could see the little Mexican cat frown and turn his back on Sam, leave him standing in the middle of the sidewalk, talking to nobody, and when Sam caught up with us again, he had a quizzical squint on his face, like he had been put down and it hurt, and he didn't know why. But I did and I nodded my head, knowingly, then sucked in air as if it were chilly to let him know that I knew exactly what had happened to him, and that it was about time too.

"Times have changed, daddy," I said and let it go at that until he hesitated going past another cab-stand and then looked at me to see what I was going to do. I shook my head for him then and walked on.

After he got put down there, he only hit on one more guy, a young cabbie, who gave him a quick shake of the head first and then said something to him, and when Sam caught up with us, he said, "They don't like being asked on the street in daylight, I guess, not by hippies anyway. This guy told me not to come around until after dark, then froze on me."

He looked at me for confirmation, but I didn't even bother to nod my head I was so pleased he was getting a taste of what I had been going through while he had been having a ball with my chick. I even wanted to drag it out a little and let it sink into his smug skull. But I was down on all counts myself, including worry about how familiar they might get down in Mazatlán, where they might start digging each other again and maybe make-out when I wasn't around. I got tired of the long walk too and didn't bother to look at the handmade goods anymore nor even get slightly amused by the pitchmen who tried to get me, us, in a good humor so we'd go inside their places and spend some money. Besides, the booze had made me lazy in the head and body by the time we got back to the corner by the first cab-stand, and I didn't even bother to check the stand and see if my old contact was there before I stepped off the curb to cross the street to my car. But Carole turned around instead of stepping down from the high curb and walked back to the mean cabbie, who was still sitting in his cab, staring at his shoe, I guess, and after jerking her hand back from the hot yellow roof, she leaned down and said something to the guy.

I waved to get her attention, to make her leave the guy alone before she got him mad enough to tell the heat on us, but she either ignored me or didn't see me, and I hurried over to stop her, and had almost gotten close enough to call her name without attracting attention when I heard her say, "We'll pay you well for it," and saw the guy suddenly sit up, heavy and dark inside, swing his head back and forth like he was looking for somebody, maybe a cop, then suddenly point past me to someone or some place across the main drag, and say something to her.

"Hurry," she said and beckoned to me, then stepped back to let me talk to the guy, who scowled when I leaned down by him but pointed a plump finger at some heavy Mexican cat in khaki brown, who had his back to us and seemed to be staring at some pictures of strippers in front of a cabaret on the other side of the main drag.

"The guy in brown?" I asked.

"Sí, sí. You talk to him. He give it to you," the cabbie said, dropping his arm, then sitting back in his seat and staring through his windshield like he had nothing more to say and I could either take his tip or forget it.

"Go hit on him, Miles," Carole said and I walked back to the corner with her, thinking about it and the cabbie and the guy he pointed out, looked back to see what the cabbie was doing, too, but he was just sitting dark as a shadow in his cab, and the guy in brown was still looking at the pictures of the strippers. So when we got to the curb again, I let her and Sam go on ahead, and after they'd gotten inside the MG, crossed the street myself. But when I was almost to the guy and could hear the band knocking out a cha-cha inside the cabaret, something about the neat cut of his clothing up close bothered me, and I turned a bit with the next step and stopped in front of the glass case next to him, pretended to look at the pictures too, then really looked at them while I looked at him.

Most of the broads were Indian chicks with flat faces and pretty eyes, browner and squatter than American chicks, but just as close to the bone. One brown-skinned chick called Swabby Sue had a black g-string the size of a band-aid over her hairless snatch and two red stars over her nipples and that's all. But the guy looked slick and O.K., like he might be dealing dope.

WHAT NOW MY LOVE

In fact, his fancy mustache was a pimp's dream, grew thick like a bandit's under his nose, and stuck out from his plump face at the pointed ends like cat's whiskers. His wavy, black hair was as full and shiny as an adolescent's too, like he took good care of it. But his shoes were what convinced me: Cuban-heeled babies with pointed toes, which was an old underworld custom dating back to the thirties, and I said, "Say?" and tugged on the guy's coat sleeve, stared at Swabby Sue to give him a chance to look at me, then followed him into the foyer of the cabaret, a small porch-like structure on the sidewalk connected to the main building, which didn't have a door, where he said, "Yeah," in a practiced way.

"Do you know where I can score some speed?" I asked, aware that I had asked for speed instead of grass, breaking my own rule of staying away from hard drugs, but conscious of the darkened nightclub to my right, too, and the crowd of Americans in it, balling it up in the daytime, rocking their shoulders to the cha-cha beat.

"Huh?" the guy said, open-eyed like he had never even heard of it before, which bothered me, and I must have really been dull-headed because I blamed the feeling on my own nerves, figured I was just worn out from no sleep and the booze, and said:

"Yeah, you, speed."

"Speed?" the guy said and pointed at himself. "Meee?"

"Yeah, you speed!" I said and wanting to skip all the trouble explaining in Spanish, I cocked an imaginary hypo between my fingers, aimed the needle at the bend of my arm where the big vein was and

snapped the plunger in with my thumb, repeating,
"Speed"!, then almost fainted when the guy grabbed
my hand, twisted it behind my back in a wristlock,
spun me around, slammed me against the stucco wall
of the foyer, flashed a badge in my face with his free
hand, and said, "Me, ponk? You mean me?"

"Pop-pop-pop, thump-thump, boom-boom,"
went the conga drum and the bartender in his white
jacket and tie looked over at me, then grabbed a
cloth and started wiping the bar, which made the
American chick sitting in front of him look over at
me too, look again, then pretend she didn't see anything either as the combo went into a rising chorus.
The only other person in the whole place who
seemed to notice what had happened was a slender
Mexican cat about twenty-five with pink acne-lumps
all over his brown face and neck, who was dressed
like a drugstore version of an American cowboy in
a white ten-gallon hat, black stovepipe riding pants
and shirt, and gleaming, nearly yellow riding boots,
and who stepped into the foyer from the nightclub
to watch when the cop put his badge away and
pulled out a pair of handcuffs.

"No, no," I said, blocking the cuffs with my free
hand, catching the cold metal claw in my palm. "I
was only teasing you."

"Teasing?" the cop said. "You kidding," and he
raised the cuff to hook it over my wrist again, but I
blocked it again, and said:

"A joke. This was a joke."

"A joke?" the bull said and cocked his head to see
my face better.

"Yeah. A joke. I knew you were a *policia*. That's why I did it."

"A jo-oke!" the bull said, frowning, the tips of his mustache sticking out from his open mouth, then put more pressure on my wrist to turn me more toward him so he could see me better. But I met his stare with some steady eyes of my own, using the fact deep within me that I really didn't want speed for the courage to do it, and he kept frowning, but he quit staring and relaxed his grip on my wrist a little too, though he kept it twisted up by my shoulder blades.

"*Sí. Yo comprendo,*" I said, meaning I comprehended, but also showing the cat when I had him unsure of himself that I wasn't one of those typical Americans who comes on down below the border and forces the little brown people to speak his language if they want his buck, and I would have told him I was a spic too if it would have helped.

The bull let my hand come down behind my back, though he still held loosely onto my wrist, after I spoke to him in Spanish. He looked at my face again when I could stand straight up as if he wanted to see it in a normal way. His own head was lowered, the points of his mustache poking up. And I forced myself to loosen up all over so that every nerve in my body was relaxed, my weight sagging, and my face soft, without fear. Though inside my chest, I was still humming and very alert, watching his face until he said, "Come with me. We'll go have a little talk," and laid his arm across my shoulders like a buddy, dug his fingers into my right shoulder muscle, and led me out of the foyer and onto the sidewalk only a few cars from my MG.

The cowboy dude followed us onto the sidewalk, high heels clicking, then watched as the cop took me to the corner, where I could only see oil spots in the dust across the street where the cab had been, though I was glad that the cabbie had split and wouldn't have told on him anyway, if only so there wouldn't be two stories to worry about, his and mine, since I was going to have to talk my ass off to save myself anyway. I was just as glad, too, that my car had been parked on the other side of the cabaret entrance so I didn't have to go by Carole and Sam with the bull, and I hoped they hadn't seen me, and wouldn't try to join us.

"We're going to have a nice talk, me and you," the bull said, keeping his arm around me like a good friend, the cowboy dude still following, and took me around the corner and down the block to an old car, late thirties maybe, handpainted a dull black, directly across from the jai-alai games, where he made me stand right next to him as he unlocked the door, and watched me as he put the key in the lock, ready to leap on me if I tried to run, then told me to get in from his side.

It was hot inside the car and the old upholstery gave off a dusty stink like old shoes which made it that much harder for me to breathe with my breath already shortened from the heat and fear, and it panicked me a little bit, since I didn't want to have to worry about air while I was fighting for my freedom, and I asked him if I could roll the window down.

"Sure. Get yourself comfortable," he said and stretched out his legs, leaned a bright shoe on a brake pedal, pulled up his neatly pressed pants by their creases to free the cloth strain around the knees, then asked, "Let me see your arms."

His mustaches twitched, though, when he saw how fast I pulled my sleeves up and how clean my arms were, not a trace of a scar on either of them, and never would have either because I'd never stick a needle in them. He nodded so I'd pull my sleeves down, twirled the tip of a mustache and looked up at the old-fashioned, beige cloth ceiling like he was thinking hard, then suddenly jabbed his finger at me and said, "You ever been in the little green house?"

"What green house?" I asked, frowning as if I was really confused and wasn't even scared, though I knew damn well what green house and *was* scared. I had seen that one-story jail at a busy intersection in the eastern part of town, with paddy wagons pulled up to the doors and blue-uniformed cops hanging around it the first time I had ever been in TJ years before, and I had seen it nearly every time since too, though I was aware they had another jail besides, and knew that they sold pot and whores inside it and didn't let you out until you paid a big bribe, which was called a fine, even if it took you years to scrape it up.

"The green house is the jail where you're going and where you'll have to stay until Sergeant Anderson comes over from San Diego to investigate your case. That will take at least a week."

"A week?" I said and was scared and let it show.

94

"But this was only a joke. I haven't done anything. Don't put me in jail."

"You asked me for speed. What do you mean 'haven't done anything'?" he said, all heavy black brows and stiff mustaches like he was mad, then when I didn't answer back or deny my guilt, he flicked the tip of the rubber floor mat with his pointed toe, stalled for dramatic effect, to scare me while he figured out what to do next, and I figured I better help him out, if I wanted to stay out, and I asked:

"What can I do not to go?"

He grinned then, and the tips of his mustache stuck far out past his cheeks as he turned completely around on the seat to face me and said, "Give me twenty bucks and you're free."

6

WITH THE COP'S WARNING TO GET OUT
of town or go to jail in my head, I hurried up the
street to the main drag, holding my back in, like the
cat was sneaking up behind me, which was pre-
posterous, and yet that's how scared I felt. But I felt
conspicuous too when I turned the corner and saw
some tourists come out of the cabaret, feared they
might have seen the guy nab me, and was feeling
like an unwashed dopefiend hippie anyway, with a
slight bristle on my face from not having shaved in
over twenty-four hours, and I avoided looking at
them. Then Carole surprised me by smiling at
me when I got close to the car, and I suddenly
realized how bouncy my step was and that I was a
little exhilarated from having just beaten a bona fide
bust, not a rumble, but a true bust, handcuffs and
all, in which I had committed an unbelievable act:
tried to score speed from a bull and walked away
from it. So she must have seen the spring in my step
in spite of the serious expression I assumed was on
my face, and her thin lips twisted down in disbelief
when I got in, kicked the motor over, started backing out, and said, "No," when she asked, "Did you
make it?"

WHAT NOW MY LOVE

"After all that trouble?" Sam asked.

"All that trouble was a bust, daddy," I said, shifting into low gear. "The guy was a cop."

"A cop?"

"A cop," I said, "and he shook me down for twenty bucks and told me to get out of town. What happened to the cab driver?"

"He split by the time you and that guy, that cop, stepped into the nightclub," Sam said and grinned. "He sent you into a cop, huh? Sort of a freakish thing to do."

"I told you he might do that when we first hit on him. Remember?" I said, and shifted into second gear to make the light, turned the corner, and headed in the general direction of the highway that led to points east, but still wanted to make my point and said, "I told you guys from the front that the cabbie might put the heat on us, and you were too stubborn to believe me."

"You mean me? Is that it?" Carole said, staring at me, her narrowed eyes visible through her dark glasses.

"Sure. You got him mad, and I almost went to jail," I said and turned right again to take a street parallel to the main drag, get heading east right away, and didn't say anything else about it and neither did she, though I could tell she was simmering by the looks she kept giving me out of the corner of her eye.

But the street I took was unpaved, and I had to slow down and drive around big holes in it and through wide sweeps of dust stirred up by cars ahead of me, and by the first block, my hood was coated a dusty red, and I started looking for a paved road going in any direction and by the second block I turned off onto a dirt street anyway, which at least looked flat, not like an obstacle course, and Carole asked, "Where are you going?"

"To Mexicali and the mainland, baby. Any place but this town," I said.

"You said we could score here!" she said, turning and poking her head out at me, her cheeks flushed at my breaking my word. But I got mad too and shouted back:

"Do you need to get us all busted before you stop? I almost went to jail a few minutes ago, you callous bitch!"

She sat back against her door, stunned, but only for a moment, then raised up to say something, looking down on me with her mouth open, but Sam said, "Hold it! Hold it!" and touched her arm, for the first time that I didn't mind, to stop her, and when she caught her breath instead of speaking, watching him, he said, "Why not pull over at that café there, Miles, so we can have a beer and calm down and talk about it. The guy's got to give you time to get out of town. He's not going to like it on the streets for a while himself."

Which made sense and I said O.K. and pulled slowly over to a small sidewalk café, with tables and chairs out on a stone veranda, and not a customer in them, and when we walked over and sat down, I knew why. Most of the chairs were of different colors and styles and the rickety tables were all second-hand jobs with tack heads sticking up through the worn oilcloth, and the only waitress was a broad-hipped, little brown chick in a house-dress, who didn't greet us when we came in or say hello when we ordered a round of beers, either.

Carole was still in a bad mood, too. Her eyes were pink-rimmed when she took off her glasses and laid them on the table. Her hands trembled when she poured her dark *Dos Equis* beer into her glass and raised it to her mouth to drink. But I shook, too. My beer bottle clicked on the glass rim like a drum roll when I tried to pour from it, and I shook so bad when I picked up the glass that I had to wait a moment and relax before I could drink from it, as if all my taut nerves broke loose when I was really away from the cop, and I couldn't do anything about it. They both noticed but didn't say anything and I didn't either. It helped prove my point about how I felt on taking another chance besides.

We were all quiet for a while, sipping on our beer, staring into our glasses when we weren't swallow-ing, feeling the effects of no sleep, booze, the long drive, the strain of trying to score, of being hunted, which put us on edge, and for me, the letdown after a crisis. The noises of the main drag sounded far away and insignificant and I wasn't in the mood to bargain with the little paper boy who leaned on the stone rail of the veranda and asked, "San Diego paper, mister," and I glanced at him, noticed that his pants were so short for his body that his legs were bare from the knees to his dirty toes, and his crotch pulled up tight between his legs. But when I started to wave him away, he held up the paper and the headline brought me out of my seat.

COP KILLED IN DOPE RAID, it said, and I

snatched the paper out of his hand, shook my head in apology for frightening him as I dug in my pocket for some money, then gave him a quarter, moved my beer, and spread the paper out on the table.

"What's wrong?" Carole asked, but jumped out of her seat too, with Sam, who scraped his chair back, when they saw the headlines, and we all leaned over the table to read.

"Daryl 'Hutch' Hutchison, a member of a motor-cycle gang, shot and killed an undercover narcotics agent, disguised as a hippie, when the State Narcotics Bureau and members of the San Francisco vice squad raided a house on Waller Street in the Haight-Ash-bury district of San Francisco with warrants to arrest the occupants for running an 'acid factory' and selling LSD," it read and also stated that several unidentified customers and one of the alleged dealers, Sam Gambarini, had escaped, the dealer with several thousand dollars of marked money.

Sam rolled his eyes and gave us a wry smile, then said, "I'm surprised they didn't say they broke up a million dollar ring. I've only got two thousand of that fuzz's money. Not a penny more."

"It doesn't make any difference how much it was. Let's knock off these beers and get the hell out of here," I said and picked up my beer and started to drink it down when Carole said, "What for?"

"To get deeper into Mexico and past the interior checkpoints on the mainland—the last one's about fifty miles in—and keep them from catching us, that's what."

"Damn you, Miles. You're so paranoid, it's crazy," she said, nearly shouting, both of her hands on her hips, "It just said that none of the customers were identified. Nobody's told them you hit that agent. He's dead. He'll never tell them. I want to get high right now. This whole trip is turning into a horrible bummer."

I set my beer down and started to tell her off, let her know what I thought about her wanting to get high, when I saw the waitress look up from inside the restaurant, where she was sweeping the floor, her widely spaced eyes chinked with interest, then look back down when she saw me notice her, and Sam, taking advantage of my hesitation, said, "Listen, man. I can go back to that corner where the cabbie told me to come back tonight, and tell him that we've got to make it now or not at all."

"And we'll get hungup again and run the streets until that cop catches me or one of you gets busted," I said, disregarding the waitress, though I could see her standing motionless inside, holding on to her broom, her dark face lowered, but still watching. "And they know who you are and that you copped big in San Diego. So there's a fair chance that they'll send a bulletin down here if we haven't gotten past the checkpoints, and they'll bust us at one of them or even here in TJ." I jabbed my finger at him. "This is murder now, man, not any little sales charge. And it's even worse than that. It's a cop-killing. And they don't like that stuff. Even the Mafia doesn't do that, only small-time punks, sometimes a professional bank robber. I want to get out of this fucking town right now. We're too hot to take any chances."

"Shit!" Carole said, and slammed her glass down

on the table, but it bounced, spilled beer on the paper, and dropped off the table edge and broke on the stone floor of the veranda before I could catch it.

"Shiiit!" she said again, her teeth showing as she dragged out the word, and she seemed to stand out from her surroundings with the hot sun on her, the wall of the building behind her, the beer-soaked paper on the table before her, like some two-dimensional paper cutout, some weird figure in a dream hovering above me, bent over still from grabbing for the glass, her teeth blaming and contemptuous, and suddenly tense and strong with anger, I felt my hand whip out and crack her across the face, send her staggering sideward, into the table next to us, knocking over a sauce bottle in the middle of it, her eyes glazed and stone still for a few seconds, until the first shock passed, then they closed as if she was going to cry and she covered her cheek with her hand, and leaned on the table, her hair falling over her face.

With her bent over the table like that and whipped, I remembered where I was, the danger, and I saw the waitress again, scowling at me from inside in the shade, and I squatted down and started picking up the pieces of glass, to show the woman I wasn't just a fuck-up, so she wouldn't call the police, and to busy myself too, both of my hands shaking, afraid to look up and see if Carole was crying.

"Did you have to hit her, man?" Sam asked, surprising me with his courage. But I was ready to blast him too if he messed with me, and cupping all the glass fragments in my left hand, both hands still shaking, I said:

"What d'you mean?"

"Do you think it was necessary, even if she did wise-off, when the odds against them putting out a pick-up on me in TJ only a day after the scene are so far out?" he said, cautious but persistent, and because he was willing to say that she had asked for it, I listened. "Those cops slept good last night, Miles. They had the killer."

He looked straight down at me, squinting a little in the sunlight, but looking more serious for it, sensible, and I quit picking up the glass fragments and stood up when the waitress came out on the veranda with her broom and dustpan, a dark frown on her dark face at the behavior of the gringos, which was ironic to me since I probably had more Spanish blood in me than she did and wasn't anything but a synthetic white man in America anyway. But I kept quiet until she had swept up all the glass, said, " '*Spensa me*," to her as she walked away, and looked at Carole again, who still held her hand to her cheek, but was looking at me through some parted strands of her hair with calm, almost soft, blue eyes, and I was sorry and wanted to say something to her, but spoke to Sam instead, with all my anger gone, wanting to make up with both of them: "How much time do you want?"

"Not more than a half hour. I'll go right back to the guy, and if he can't make it, I'll come right back, and we'll get out of here. I'm not eager to get busted either, and besides it's easier to score up here on the border than down on the mainland."

My limbs felt weak again, though, and I hesitated before I answered, knowing that it was a warning not to do it, but I could see Carole still standing by the table, still holding her hand to her cheek where I had hit her, watching me with mild, blue eyes, and I said to him but kept looking at her: "We'll meet at that yellow church over there." I pointed at it but looked back at Carole. "It's only a few blocks away and there won't be any tourists and cops around to look out for. We'll see you there. But don't bring the pusher to the car. I don't want anybody we score from to see it."

She smiled.

7

TJ DIDN'T LOOK QUAINT TO ME ON THE
way to the church to meet Sam with Carole, not
anymore. The Moorish-style houses that belonged to
the better off Mexicans, with the wrought-iron gates
and barred windows to keep the poor out seemed
run down and crumbling, and I wasn't even amused
by the barefooted kids playing in the streets, who
shook their fists and cussed me out in Spanish
when they had to move over to let the MG by,
then dragged their feet through the dust, just
barely out of the way of my tires. Dust floated in
through the windows, too, all the way, and I was
sweating so badly that my turtle neck stuck to my
back and my underarms tickled from the trickling
drops. The roads were bad as usual and I had to
creep in low gear through a series of holes and
boulders big as the front of the car, and cringed at
the scrape of my muffler when I dropped in and out
of the dry rain gulleys that ran like natural gutters
through intersections. But Carole bothered me the
most.

She didn't like the dust at all and would roll her
window up when we went through big clouds stirred
up by cars in front of us, then brush impatiently at

her dress with her green scarf to get the dust off, though she didn't try to take it out on me. She sat in her bucket seat like there was a temporary truce between us, would glance over at me every once in a while and stare at me for a few seconds through her dark glasses as if she were appraising me, and when I'd turn and meet her stare, she'd smile but in a distant way. Once, close to the church, she touched her palm to her cheek, very gently, as if it still tingled from the slap, then looked at me again, out of the corner of an eye, a near smile on her lips, which could have meant anything, because she didn't talk, at all. Not that I felt like talking but her silence was a put-down. She was getting her way after all, and I could even detect a haughty air in her silence, the way she sat in her seat without bothering to speak to me now that Sam went to score, as if there was weakness in my pity for her and shame for myself, for giving in after I had already hit her. But not a total put-down, the slap had hurt too much for that. In fact, sometimes her eyes were even bright through the glasses when she glanced at me, as if in admiration, as if I were a worthy foe and a guy she was willing to give some nookie to, after a fight, that is.

It was almost too much for me—I liked to get along with my broad not battle with her, and I was near to the point where I didn't care if she split with Sam, and was even considering taking off with my last ten dollars and going back to the States, where I could find jobs to support myself at least, and let them catch a bus to Mazatlán. I wanted the chick but not at the cost of my life, and when I saw the market place scene in front of the church, I snorted bitterly at myself for being so naive as to think the church would be a quiet, safe spot, frequented by pious people in a hustlers' town.

I couldn't get closer than a block to it there were so many thousands of people buying and selling in the square in front of it. There were so many booths and foot peddlers, who had just dropped their wares in the dust and set up shop, that even in the late afternoon, and they must have been there since early morning, the whole street in front of the church looked like a bazaar. And they sold everything to each other that they sold to Americans too, plus fruit and vegetables, raw meat and live chickens, which kept the constant noise of bickering humans and squawking animals at an hysterical pitch. Even the steps of the church were crowded with salesmen, selling every type of product, right up to the front doors, which nobody used, and after I pulled over to the side of the road, which didn't have a sidewalk, I braced my elbows on the steering wheel, cupped my chin in my hand, and, worn out, stared out the dirty window at the frenzied market place, and wasn't even surprised when I saw the peak of a white cowboy hat bob up the church steps next to a tall guy in a white Nehru jacket, then surface completely at the top of them and Sam shade his eyes with his hand and look around for the car.

"I think Sam brought back the buddy of the cop who busted me today," I said, shaking my head and snorting through my nose again. "He's probably got the cop with him too."

"That's not true," Carole said, leaning down to see better. "Where is he? Who's he with?" Then she evidently saw him because she opened her door and stood up in the street, where, looking about a half a foot taller than everybody around her and easily twice the size of the car, she waved her green scarf to attract his attention, and got the attention of most of the people around us, who turned around to watch her and see what she was up to, and I said, "Sit down, Carole," just as Sam waved back and, followed by the white cowboy hat, hopped down the church stairs, and disappeared in the crowd at the foot of them, headed in our direction.

Muttering to myself that if I got through this score scene without getting busted, I was going to split with or without Carole, I told her to get back in the car so I could turn it around, which stopped her protest, then backed it up to the corner, and sat in my seat watching for them in the side view mirror but facing ahead so the guy, when he got to us, would have less chance of recognizing me. Though I didn't really think the pimple-faced dude in the cowboy hat had brought the cop with him, because the cop would have never let Sam get out of grabbing range in this crowd and I would have seen him up on the church steps with them. That meant, then, that I could still get out of things even if the cowboy cat was an undercover man. They'd have to catch me with the dope to bust me, and I could ditch the guy when he went to score.

"He can make it but he needs a ride," Sam said through my window when he reached us. But since I sat low in my seat and wouldn't answer, he went around to Carole's door with the dude and tried to fit himself and the guy into the back seat while

WHAT NOW MY LOVE

Carole waited outside, standing propped on one leg, one hand on an outflung hip, the other hanging down past her thigh clear to her miniskirt's hemline, the scarf dangling from it, while about a hundred Mexicans from young men in washed-out clothes to grandmothers in widows' weeds stared at her, until Sam finally made enough room for their legs back there by stuffing the sleeping bags into the fastback window with the rest of our gear and they all got in.

"He usually drives cab and wouldn't need a ride, but this is his day off. He says it won't take him but a few seconds when we get to the house," Sam said, trying to get friendly with me, clean up for himself after he brought the guy back with him and let about five thousand people see us all in the car together.

"Which way?" I asked, driving down the bumpy street without turning around, to let him know that I didn't like it even if I had to go along with it, though I looked at the guy in the rear view mirror, and watched him try to put on his tall hat in the car, which was impossible, for even *his* head nearly touched the ceiling back there, while Sam sat with his head bent, his chin touching his chest and his knees tucked up by his chin. Finally the guy gave it up, put the hat on his knee and twisting his mouth down to the side in a sneer and talking through his nose, to come on hard, said, "Turn right, mannn, and go straight across the main street for a few blocks. I'll let you know what to do then."

Ugly, pink lumps covered his whole brown face from the low hairline of his stiff hair, greased down with pomade and sweat from his hat, to his fancy, black shirt collar with gold stitching, and I detested the cat for giving us the talking-through-the-nose bit and the wise-guy sneer to come on hard and let us know how hip he was—dressed like an American cowboy, that is. But I didn't say anything or act hostile in any way either because I didn't want him to be able to positively identify me, even if he had already recognized me, which was very possible the way the cat kept staring at me from the back seat, which I caught by glancing in the mirror, and it looked like he was going to ask me about it because he studied me, his eyes chinked, his bumpy forehead all furrowed for a few seconds. But I gave him the back of my head so he wouldn't get a chance to get familiar and Sam took his attention away by asking, "How much is a paper?"

"A fin," the dude said, sneering.

"A what?" Carole asked, leaning against the door so she could see him.

"Five dollars," the guy said with a grin and snorted as if she was incredibly stupid, and though I would have liked to have punched the cat for it, I began to worry less and less about his being a cop. He turned me off too bad. Undercover cops ingratiate themselves, try to make you like them so they can put you in jail, lock you up. This guy was working too hard to impress us in a different way. He was a thief, and he asked, like he was giving them away free, "How many you want?"

"Two apiece," Carole said, and when I couldn't help looking at her, letting the guy see my profile, she added, "One for later," and I got brought down even more. They didn't have the slightest intention of getting any grass, and I didn't want to ask the cat for it myself, even allow him to talk to me, so he could never testify to what I said later.

"Six?" the guy asked, and Carole looked at me, knowing I didn't use it, yet wondering, seeming to be all dark glasses for a couple of seconds, then shook her head and said, "Four," to the guy, but still looking at me. Yet she still didn't ask the guy for grass, and I wondered if she was trying to strike back at me for the slap, though her face was calm and showed no malice.

But the guy wasn't paying attention to where we were going either and while he made sure that he looked cool in the back seat with the right sneer on his face, he let me drive into a pit of dust in the middle of the street that had looked like solid ground, and one of my rear tires sank down in it and spun a couple of times. So I had to stop, rock back and forth and then creep slowly out of it in first gear, and the guy still didn't bother to say anything. Then when I finally got myself out of the trap and made it to an intersection without any more trouble, he waited until I was nearly across it before he said, "Turn here," and I sent up a big cloud of dust at twenty miles an hour making the turn. But after I straightened out again, and was mad enough to say something to him about his directions, he leaned forward, poked his arm into the front seat, and pointed at a low, unpainted shack about a block ahead, which sat alone on the edge of a wide field of weeds and cactus, and everybody in the car got quiet, not just me—we were all watching the house.

As we drew near it, I scanned the neighborhood

111

to see if there were any plainclothes bulls hanging around, and though I didn't see a single person, I still slowed down to give the house a good look over before I pulled up by it. Often the slightest and smallest thing out of the ordinary can tell you if there's something wrong and sometimes *what's* wrong too. The house didn't look like it had been used in years. Warped slats peeled out from the walls where they had covered the cracks between the un-painted boards, and the house even tipped a little toward the front porch, which had broken floor-boards and a barbed-wire railing, no steps, and a dirt path through a yard of weeds to the barbed-wire fence that separated it from the dusty road. But, most of all, I didn't like the way the windows were boarded up, meaning nobody lived in the house. So why would we be going inside? To park out in front would be, at the very least, conspicuous and probably very dangerous, so I drove past without stopping, and Carole asked, "What are you doing, Miles?"

"He means this house, Miles," Sam said.

"Right here," the dude said.

"Sure," I said and slowed down even more but still kept moving.

"Right here, Miles!" Carole said as a two-toned green, '41 Cadillac with two men in it came around the curve in the road about a block ahead of us and the dude yelled:

"Don't stop! Don't stop! Keep moving!" and knocked his hat off his knees and ducked his face down by them.

WHAT NOW MY LOVE

Keeping my car at the same speed I was already traveling so as not to act suspicious, I drove straight toward the Cadillac, getting a good look at the guys inside, both bulls, both wearing dark glasses and sportcoats, both beefy like cops get, and both staring at me. But one was a big, blond American and the other was a Mexican Federalé with a mustache, and I knew that times had changed forever. But I drove right past them and even looked at them in a naturally curious way, like any sight-seeing tourist, driving through their dust while they drove through mine, and even glanced out the side window at them when I made the turn with the road to see what they were going to do, but they neither stopped to turn around and follow us nor bothered to slow down by the house, and, no longer worried about the dude getting a good look at my face—he wasn't a cop; maybe a stool pigeon at best—I said, "They kept moving, man. Can they circle around and cut us off on this road?"

His head bobbed up and he glanced out Sam's window to make sure they weren't following us before he answered, "No. They have to go a long way before they'll hit a cross street," then put his cowboy hat back on his knees and started squeezing nervously at a pink lump on his cheek. "We can't go back there, though. Not if they're watching it that close. Those are tough cops, man. And with that American along that Federalé won't let you go so fast as that TJ cop did today. No *mordida* with him. Not for small fry like us."

"*Mordida?*" Carole asked. "What's that?"

"Bribery," I said, as much to keep the guy from wising-off to her for being stupid as to give her an answer.

"How do you know him?" Sam asked the dude.

"I saw him get shook down by a TJ cop today," the dude said, smiling, then examined his fingers and rubbed them together to get rid of the pus.

"He was in the carbaret when the bull grabbed me and he watched the whole thing. I'm surprised you guys didn't see him. He followed us to the car," I said, since they were both waiting for an explanation. "Where can I drop you off?" I asked the dude and kept the car headed in the general direction of the main drag.

"Drop him off?" Carole said and turned her dark glasses on me, ready to fight again, as if she had already forgotten about the slap I gave her. But I kept my eyes on the road and didn't answer back, not about to take my mind off getting rid of the guy by arguing with her, and it surprised her. She paused, expecting me to shout back so she could attack me, and Sam said to the dude:

"Can't you make it any place else?"

"I don't know about now, mannn. I'd have to go downtown and see. But I can make it tonight around eight or eight-thirty."

"Let's go downtown then," Carole said.

"Hell no," I answered. "I'm not looking any more. This town is red hot. Mexican and American bulls working in teams. Trucks going around town to warn people about drugs. Man, every move we've made has come up a bummer. The handwriting's

on the wall: we're going straight to jail if we keep
this up. And you know what that means," I warned,
without going into details in front of the dude.

"I don't care! It's better than this constant bummer!" Carole yelled, getting her chance to attack me
finally, her breath strong from the booze, though she
didn't bother me very much, and I wasn't going to
answer her. But when Sam said, "Let's give this
guy one more chance, Miles," I jammed my foot
down on the brake, skidded to a halt on the dirt
road, sending up a cloud of dust, and shouted:

"Fuck all you guys. And you, you fucking bitch,
you self-centered cunt, don't give a shit about nothing or nobody, you can go get as high as you want,
I'm splitting and right now."

That shocked her. She fell back against her door
with wide eyes, her mouth open but silent, and Sam
said, "Don't be so hard on the chick, man. She just
wants to live."

"What the fuck do you know about it, man?
You're worse than she is, only more naive. This
broad has been using you the whole trip, like right
now, to play off against me and get her own way.
Because she knows that if she pushes me too far,
I'll split on her. I've done it before."

"You're jealous," Carole screamed, willing to risk
another slap, and the Mexican dude grinned and
squeezed a lump on his chin, evidently amused by the
sight of the big, blond, American chick shouting at
the little American cat like that. Mexican women
might run the show at home but they keep quiet in
public so a guy won't lose face. But his grin vanished

when I glared at him, and then I screamed back at her, my own voice ringing in my ears, my face hot with anger:

"You Goddamn rights I am. I care about my broad and I'll break the guy's ass that messes with her, if she wants me. But if she doesn't, then I'm not hanging around, and that goes for right now! I'll take off with my crummy ten dollars but I'll go."

"Go ahead then," Carole said, but in a sobered voice and her face sagged. "We can do better without you. Our money'll go twice as far."

"Tell me where you want out, baby," I said, but Sam said:

"Don't split, Miles. We need your car and you need our money, man."

"I don't need this bitch at all," I said, looking at her and not at him. "I can do great without her. She's caused the whole goddamn thing, from my staying so long in the pad in San Francisco that I finally ended up blasting the bull, to all the bummers that have happened today. And she'll fuck us up further down too, if she doesn't do it here."

She closed her eyes and made a tight mouth when I said that, as if it really hurt her, and I felt a little sorry for her and didn't say anything else, and Sam took advantage of the momentary calm to say, "Look, man," to me, but then catch himself, as if he thought better of what he had in mind, and spoke to the dude instead: "Can you score some grass right now?"

"Easy to get as cigarettes," the dude said, pinching his face, and Sam glanced at Carole and then at me and said:

WHAT NOW MY LOVE

"Let's go score some grass right now and get right on the highway to Mexicali. O.K., Miles?"

I wouldn't look at him when he asked me nor at Carole nor the dude either. I stared out the window instead, though I hardly saw the adobe houses around me, the dusty street, nor even the bull ring sticking up to the left of me a few miles away, hazy in the late afternoon. I was aware of the coat of dust over my green hood though, and the heat, and I hooked a finger under my turtle neck to let some body steam out, let the neckband snap back and said, "O.K.," then propped my arms on the steering wheel and leaned heavily down on it, disgusted with myself for giving in, particularly since it was for grass, which I wanted and Sam knew it. But I warned, looking over my shoulder at him: "But this is it, dad. If we don't make it on the first try, we drop him off and drive right out of town."

Both Carole and Sam had unhappy frowns on their faces until the dude stuck out his lower lip, nodded once, curtly, and said, "Nothing to it. Turn around right here and head back close to where we came from. I'll show you guys how easy it is when you're with the right man."

That made Carole and Sam smile and settle back in their seats while I turned the car around in the rutted road and headed back toward the fields on the northern edge of town, but noticed the dude staring at me in the rear view mirror, and though I wanted to tell him off for his rudeness, I asked, "How'd you learn to speak English so well, man?" barely able to keep the hatred out of my voice.

"In the joint, mannn," he said, dragging the an-

swer out to a sneer, his upper lip then peaking near
his pocked nostril on one side. "I did three years in
San Quentin for dealing grass. Then they kicked me
out of the country."

He seemed to really be proud of hitting the joint
and he sneered once again, the left side of his lip
trembling clearly to me in the mirror, and I would
have liked to have puffed it up for real with my fist,
but followed his directions without showing how I
felt, and we once more made a tortuous trip down
side streets, sinking down to the hubcaps a couple of
times in the powdery dust that covered everything in
town, in most of Mexico for that matter, and I
really got annoyed at the guy for it, because he was
busy showing some knife scars on his brown belly to
Carole and Sam, bragging about all the dangerous
battles he'd had in San Quentin and only giving me
directions in his off-hand way, and I was just about
to tell the motherfucker to talk to me in a decent
manner when he suddenly sat up, buttoned his shirt,
looked around, saw that we had reached the last
road along the northern edge of town, where there
were only weed and cactus fields clear to the border
hills, and pointed to an unpainted building on the
left that looked like a big, unused barn, about a
block or so away, which sat on the edge of a field by
itself, across from a row of wooden shacks, patched
all over with different types and shapes of tin and
boards, and said, "Right there, man. Bing-bang.
Be right back."

A large crowd of Mexicans in gray workclothes
hung around the big barn door, which had a smaller
house-sized door next to it, through which I must

have seen three or four guys go in and out before I
even got close to the barn, and about ten old cars
parked out in front. The place looked so wide open
that for the first time since we'd tried to score, including Sam's pad, I wasn't uptight about making
the dope scene, and I didn't even bother to drive by
the barn first, but pulled up right in front of the
place and turned off the motor, which are two
things I never do until I'm sure there aren't any bulls
around, then sat with my body sort of simmering in
sweat, my mind dulled, and my eyesight as wavering
and unsure as the heat waves that warped the shapes
of the houses and fence posts around me, and heard
the dude say, "Give me the money, man, and I'll
get you a good deal."

Sam went into his pocket and pulled out his big
wad, which wasn't a wise thing to do in front of the
guy, then pulled a twenty-dollar bill off that and
gave it to the dude, who stuffed it into the slit of his
front pocket and got out Carole's side without
Sam or Carole even telling him how much grass they
wanted, which was the third mistake by my book,
the second being you never give a dealer the money
until he's given you the weed. But I didn't say anything to either of them about it, because I didn't care
enough to argue.

They seemed to be worn out too, though, and
none of us talked while the guy was gone. Carole
could have been a guy next to me for all that was
between us at the time. Sam was perfectly silent in
the back seat. And I gazed, without really looking,
at the alley that passed for a street and the homemade
houses that were built mostly of patches of tin and

scrap lumber, most of it stolen from signs, I guessed, since some of the sun-blistered letters still showed. There were also piles of ashes and rotting garbage between the shacks and the outside toilets, and a permanent odor of piss hung with the heat in the air. I was so depressed by everything in Mexico that I never once looked in the direction of the barn, which was to my right, until the dude came back to the car and opened the door to get in, had to squeeze by Carole, and I noticed that all the Mexican guys out in front were staring at us, but I still didn't care and asked the guy which way he wanted to go before I even started the car.

"Turn right with the road toward the highway; it's cooler, mannn," the dude said, sneering, and made himself comfortable in the back seat, and I almost said something wise to him but caught myself, knowing it wasn't worth the trouble since we'd be rid of him in a few minutes at most anyway.

I drove down the little alley, then turned right down a wide road, almost white with dust, that passed through acres of weeds and cactus so coated with dust they were almost white too, and headed for the highway, determined to drop the guy off as soon as he gave Sam the grass, thinking he just wanted to get away from the barn before he came up with it, and I wasn't even listening to what was going on in the back seat when I heard Sam say, "Twenty joints! Are you kidding?" and I looked over my shoulder to see the guy buttoning his shirt as if he had just taken the weed out from under it.

"When you buy in TJ, you got to pay a good price, mannn," he said to me, sneering again and spreading his orange palms. "It's hot around here. You saw those narcos. If you guys had wanted a kilo, I could have got it for you for seventy-five dollars."

"Let me see how much he gave you," I said to Sam and shook my head when I saw the roll of brown bombers, wrapped with a rubber band, in his hand, and all the resentment that had been building up in me over the whole twenty-four hours of bummer after bummer came to a head. I glared at the dude, sitting in my back seat with his white hat on his knees, his stiff, greased-down hair, and his pock-marked face twisted in a wise-guy sneer, and I warned: "Hey, man, you better come up with about a hundred times more grass than that or give my boy his money back. And you better do it quick."

But the dude just squeezed a large lump on his cheek and said, "I tol'ja, mannn, grass costs in TJ. That's all there is to it," then stared at me from under his bumpy forehead with hard, black eyes, and I knew there was no use in my trying to talk him into giving the money back since he probably thought I was the weakest one of all, the way I had given in to Sam and Carole over scoring in the first place, and I said:

"O.K., man, we'll see about that."

Carole squinted her eyes at me like she did when I told Sam off in the car leaving San Francisco. But I had too much to do to worry about what she thought and checking behind me in the side view mirror and seeing that nobody, not a car nor a person, was on the road behind me and that no one was ahead of me for the mile or so to the highway either, though I noticed a line of tourists' cars backed up from the border already, I pulled the car over to the side of the road, and made sure not to drive onto the shoulder and risk sliding down into the dust-filled ditch. Then, without bothering to say one word to anyone, let alone the dude, I leaned across the gearshift that stuck up between me and Carole and reached down to the floor by her feet and caught the wine jug by its handle with my hooked finger and fished it out from under the dashboard, the wine splashing back and forth inside, then glanced at the dude, who was all squinty-eyed and worried now, and got out of the car.

All faces inside turned to watch me as, holding the jug by the neck like a club, I stepped around the back of the car and up to Carole's door, opened it, and still without bothering to explain, told her: "Get out and stand back there out of the way," pointed behind me, refused to look at her or anyone when she got out, then pushed the back of her seat down to give me swinging room, cocked the jug over my shoulder, with a splash of wine, and leaned down in to the car with my knee braced against the door frame, and said, "Either give us back our money or come up with some more grass, if you don't want your ugly head busted with this jug, mannn," unable to resist mocking him.

"No, no, mann," the dude said and threw himself back in his seat, knocking his hat off his knees, sticking his arms out in front of him to protect himself, and Sam bunched up against his corner too, looking as scared as the dude, but I warned:

"There ain't going to be no 'no-no' you loud-talking motherfucker, unless you come up with some money and right now."

"O.K., man, O.K.," the dude said, and with one black-sleeved arm still held out in front of him, he fumbled in his tight pants pocket until he finally jerked the twenty-dollar bill out and handed it to me with the tips of his fingers, trying to stay as far away as possible, and froze that way with both arms held out in front of him when I reached down under his arms with the same hand I held the money in and tapped his front pockets to make sure he wasn't holding a blade he could stab me with when I started driving again. He winced each time but he didn't say anything, and he even kept his arms straight out when I leaned back away from him, pushed Carole's seat back in place, then straightened up outside the car and lowered the jug.

"What did you do that for?" Carole asked, but her voice was curious not condemning, and I could even see her eyes sparkle behind her glasses.

"Because he burned us," I said, feeling mean, and walked back around the car. "Get in and let's get out of here."

Once in the car again, I headed straight for the highway and saw that the line of cars I had noticed before I pulled the jug on the guy was a real Sunday-evening traffic jam of bumper-to-bumper cars from the border clear back to where our dirt road met the highway, a couple of miles distance at least. But I wasn't concerned with that. I was only concerned with what I was going to do with the dude in the back seat, who sat there with dull, black eyes and a very inoffensive face, no sneer, and feeling a little sorry for him, I said to Sam, who hadn't moved from his spot in the corner: "Take your twenty and give this guy five dollars for those joints you've got. For getting them rolled at least. That's a fair enough price."

Sam took the bill from me, shifted around in the back seat, and then came up with a five-dollar bill which he offered to the dude, who only shook his head, and wouldn't even say no. So catching the guy's eyes in the rear view mirror, I said, "Hey, man, take the money. We expect you to make something on the deal. We just don't want you burning us like we're a bunch of punks."

But the dude shook his head again and looked away so he wouldn't have to look in my eyes, and I really felt sorry for him, though I knew he was as unhappy over being humiliated after playing tough-guy as over losing the money or he would have settled for what he could get.

Yet, I still had him in my car and was getting farther and farther away from town and was so close to the highway, in fact, that I could see the Mexican peddlers in their perpetually gray clothes moving along from trapped car to trapped car, calling out: "Soo-ve-neer! Soo-ve-neer!" I also noticed that the bumper-to-bumper car line now disappeared in the orange haze of the setting sun, the shadowy lumps of the low hills between TJ and the sea, and the vague patch of low buildings and trees which was the border gate, and knew that I'd better get going toward Mexicali right away or I'd end up in some kind of trouble with nightfall: either busted again—and this time maybe for keeps—or done-in by the dude and some of his cabdriver friends. But still feeling guilty enough over the money hassle to take a chance on getting caught in town by the dude's buddies, I asked, "Where do you want off, man? We'll drop you off wherever you want."

But the dude just shook his head and looked around him when I stopped at the highway as if he didn't know what he wanted to do, and since I wasn't about to get trapped in the traffic jam, I turned right away from it and the border and east on the highway, which didn't seem to have a car on it and which disappeared in the long shadows of the small, brown, border hills, the shadows worrying me by their length. Finally, after driving for a few more blocks, I said, "We're getting farther away from town, man. You better make up your mind," and the dude suddenly said:

"Right here. Just let me off right here. This is fine."

"Right here?" I asked, seeing nothing but miles and miles of cactus on both sides of us, knowing it was a good five or six miles back to the cabaret where I had seen him and Sam must have picked him up. "We'll take you back to town, man," I said over my shoulder. "We're not going to try and hurt you. Don't worry about that."

"No, no," the dude said, meeting my eyes for a moment. "Right here is fine. Right here. Fine. Fine."

I slowed down a little then, looked back down the highway, guessed that we had come about a half mile from the traffic jam and that it would be a dusty walk to anywhere, noticed a yellow cab come out of a shadowy dip in the highway up ahead, and said, "Say, man, we won't mess with you. We'll take you into town. We just don't want you burning us."

"No, no," the dude said and leaned forward with a worried frown on his face. "Let me out right away. Let me out."

So I pulled half-off the pavement to a stop, not about to trust the dusty shoulder with the car's full weight, and told Carole to let him out, saying as she opened the door and leaned forward enough to allow him to press the back of her seat down and squeeze by: "Sure you don't want the five dollars?"

The dude didn't even bother to shake his head, just ducked it low enough to get through the door, then slid his body out, slammed the door, and started across the highway before I even pulled away, stepping sort of jerky in my side view mirror, getting tiny fast as I gained speed, but then suddenly stopped and waved his arm as if to call me back, and I stuck my head out the window to see what he wanted when the yellow cab with several men in it droned by me and slowed down to pick him up. I still wasn't worried though and watched while the passenger door opened and shut on him, but caught my breath when the cab backed up onto the shoulder to make a U-turn and come after us.

"Hey!" I said. "That off-duty cabbie friend of yours just flagged down that yellow cab that passed us with a bunch of guys in it, and they're turning around to chase us," and I hit the gas pedal hard and zoomed into high speed so fast that Carole, who had turned around to see the cab, caught her breath and turned back around in her seat to see what I was

doing, as much afraid of my driving as the cab behind us.

I was moving fast and even gloating a little, my
jaw tight with the thrill, knowing I could hit ninety
in a quarter-mile and double their speed, watching
the cab get smaller and smaller in the side view mirror until I finally lost sight of it in the orange haze
and was straining my eyes to spot it again when
Carole screamed, "Look out, Miles!" and I glanced
ahead to see a peddler standing in the middle of my
lane, with a basket of souvenirs on his back and his
arm up, waving at me to stop, with a red straw doll
in his hand, but his arm was stiff now and his mouth
was open in a scream I couldn't hear, and I jerked
the wheel to the left to miss him and hit my brakes
at the same time to keep from shooting off the opposite side of the road, but the car tipped to the right
like it would go over and I spun the wheel that way,
then back to the left and it zigzagged, then spun into
a wobbling spin, and I jammed the brake down and
held onto the wheel to keep myself from falling out
and to keep the front tires from twisting and turning us over as the rear-end of the car skidded past the
front end in a long shriek of rubber and pinging
rocks, a sweeping view of a lopsided landscape, but
kept turning completely around and swept off the
side of the road, dropped into the deep ditch still
turning and smashed broadside into the barbed-wire
fence at the bottom with a body-jarring crash and an
explosion of dust, facing our original direction.

It seemed like we sat there in the front seat for a
full minute, engulfed by dust, coughing and squinting and covering our eyes and mouths with our

hands, trying to breathe something beside the dry grit that clogged our nostrils and mouths, burned our eyes, though I remembered to reach down and turn off the key to keep the car from bursting into flames and even wondered briefly how much it would cost to have the car fixed, since Carole's whole side must have been smashed in, though she didn't seem to be hurt, and none of us even cried out, when I suddenly remembered the cab with the dude and all his friends in it and I yelled, "Sam! Get out and help me fight!"

Then, without waiting to see if he'd do it, I grabbed my keys, forced my door open and jumped out and ran around to the back of my car, shoved the key into the lock with shaking hands, flipped the fastback top up, propped it open, yelled at Sam again, who hadn't moved and whom I could have touched through the dust still swirling around the car, jerked the loose bag of tools out from under Carole's knapsack, dumped all the tools in the ditch, threw the bag down, grabbed a small brass mallet that had been furnished with the car, shouted at Sam, who had turned around to see what I was doing, to get out and grab one of the tire tools, then ran up the ditch to the highway, and watched the yellow cab pull up to a stop by the peddler, who was crouched at the side of the road with his face in his hands, about a hundred feet behind me.

All four doors flew open immediately and all the Mexicans—and there must have been about five of them—jumped out and ran around to the trunk at the back of the car to get weapons, while the dude in his cowboy hat kept shouting and waving his arms at me, and I yelled, "Sam, you better get out of that fucking car and help me fight," my heart quickening with fear when I saw how far we were from the line of tourists' cars and how quickly the Mexicans made a line across the highway in front of the cab, with knives and car tools in their hands.

"Sam!" I yelled again when the dude got in the middle of them, raised a lug wrench up above his shoulder and shouted, *"Le mato,* motherfucker! I'll kill you for sure!" and started running down the highway at me, followed by all the others, one of them in a white dress shirt without a tie, the cabdriver I think, carrying a squat jack like a big rock in his hands.

There was an anxious spasm down in my belly and a terrible weakening in my legs when they started running at me, and I knew I'd die of fear if I didn't start fighting right away, and sure I was going to die anyway, I shouted, "Well then we'll kill each other, motherfuckers," and started running at them, but aimed for the dude in the cowboy hat, watching out for his four-spoked lug wrench in case he threw it and any unusual move by any of the others, too, but running at him, running to kill him and maybe get killed with a burst of speed much faster than his pace, and it surprised him and he slowed and shouted something in Spanish, then stopped with stiff-heeled, awkward steps in his cowboy boots, and all the others, though they swept on past him for a few feet, stopped too.

But I kept running, knowing I had just gained an advantage, feeling too brave moving to risk stopping and getting scared all over again, not caring if

WHAT NOW MY LOVE

I died or not anyway, since I had nothing to lose, and I wanted to die strong at least, not cringing, and it must have showed because the dude's face twisted with shock and he braced himself with his legs apart, warned, "I'll kill you! I'll kill you!" then leaned back and threw the lug wrench like a boomerang at me.

But I broke direction with his heave and had already moved a step or two out of his aim when he let go, and the wrench missed and chipped sparks off the pavement with a clatter when it hit, and he fell down to his hands from the force of the throw, and was just pushing himself back up to a standing position when I cracked him over the head with a short, wrist-swing of the mallet, dented his ten-gallon hat in like an egg shell, and dropped him flat on his face in the middle of the road, but didn't stop there, shouted, "Yeaaaaaah! Motherrrrfuckerrrr!" with victory and leaped at the cabbie, who had already jumped back and raised the squat jack over his head with both hands to heave at me, but hesitated with scared eyes, like he was afraid he'd miss and lose his weapon like the dude did, and I leaped in on my left foot and jerked my hammer up like I was going to swing and he threw the jack, but I bounced right back off my toes with his toss to my right foot, and he missed completely and threw his arms up to protect his head as I danced back in, dropped into a crouch under his arms and smashed the mallet into his rib cage with a dull thump, and he screamed and grabbed his heart and fell over backwards onto the pavement, where he twisted around, gasping for breath, turning purple in the face, but I was already dancing on my toes toward the two guys with knives behind him, trying to make them make the first move to keep me away, but they back-stepped fast, then turned around and ran back toward the cab and didn't stop until they reached the peddler, who was now standing up and watching me with his mouth open as if he thought I was completely crazy.

I watched them for a moment to see what they were going to do when an American tourist car, passing slowly by me in the right lane, its passengers staring at me, caught my attention, and I remembered the other two Mexicans who had knives too, and I spun around with my mallet raised, ready to bring it down with a backward swing, sure the guys were sneaking up on me, but saw them slipping across the road behind another American car full of tourists, who were staring at them, and heading toward the stalled MG, Carole, who was bent over in the ditch behind it as if looking through the tools for a weapon, and Sam, who was standing by the open door with dust all over him, watching them come at him, and making no attempt to defend himself, not even warning Carole.

"Look out!" I yelled and started running down the road again to cut off the first guy, a thin, wall-eyed man in a pinstripe suitcoat and khaki work pants, a work hat, and a long knife held out in front of him, whom I had noticed when they lined up in front of the cab to charge me.

Carole heard me and straightened up to see what was wrong, then saw the guy and faced him, but Sam stood by the car door, with his hands at his sides, and watched the guy stop and look down at him from the ditch edge, then, dark-faced and gaunt, with leathery lines in his face, start edging down the ditch toward him, with the blade held out in front of him.

"Fight, Sam! Fight the guy!" I shouted and started running with every bit of energy in me, stretching my legs for longer strides, my chest out, my arms pumping, my head high, my hair blowing back, shouting hoarsely: "Fight him, Sam! Fight him! Fight him!"

But Sam just stood there, chalky with dust and fear, and Carole looked at me, then at Sam, then shouted, "Fight him, Sammmmm!" and threw her dark glasses away and charged the guy, screaming, "You dirty coward, you dirty sonofabitch!" and intercepted him coming down the ditch, grabbed his coat and clawed at his face, made him take a step back, then trip, and fell on him, still clawing and screaming, half-words, half-shrieks, which were garbled by her anger and his Spanish curses, while he tried to push her away with one hand and watch me charge down on him too, looking at both of us and neither of us, it seemed, with his walleye, which was wide and scared and desperate, and he suddenly screamed himself, and jabbed her in the body with the blade, and she jerked straight up, stared at me, almost to her, with her pale eyes, her mouth open, then grabbed her breasts and fell over backwards into the dust, and I didn't see her again because I leaped into the ditch as she fell and smashed the blade out of his hand when he jabbed at me, then clubbed him on the shoulder when he turned

over on his hands and feet to run, then clubbed him
in the middle of his back, between his shoulder
blades, as he jumped away and dropped him,
hunched up, in the ditch by the front fender, his
arms over his head, then clubbed him in the back
again and he groaned, then smashed at the protecting
hands over his head and knocked his head under the
bumper by the front wheel, but he still had his
hands over it, and I started to club him again, to beat
him to death for stabbing my broad when I remembered the other guy, who had stopped in the middle
of the road when he saw me start running at his
friend, and sure he was about to kill me, I twisted
around, swinging blindly backhand with the mallet, denting my car door in, but saw him at the top
of the ditch on the shoulder as I spun around and
started up the ditch after him, without pausing, sure
that I was going to get him now that he had missed
his chance to get me with my back turned.

But the guy started running when I did, across the
road, into the right lane, and I wondered where he
was going until I reached the roadway and saw
another yellow cab full of Mexicans pull up halfway
between me and the first cab and the doors all open at
once, but close again, without anybody getting out
when they saw how fast I was chasing the guy,
how badly I wanted him, and he changed direction
and headed toward the parked cab, shouting over his
shoulder at me in a squeaky voice: *"Le mato! Le
mato!"* and waving his knife to scare me.

But I was long past being scared and kept running
after him, passed the second cab quickly and caught
up with him so fast that he stopped and turned

around and swung his knife in a wild, wide arch to keep me away, but I jumped back with his swing, then danced in and clubbed him over his head while his own arm was still wrapped around him, buckled his knees and dropped him into a sitting position on the highway, his eyes glazed, his face white, no blood showing, and noticed how young he was, maybe sixteen or seventeen, then glanced once more at the guys by the parked cab to see if they wanted any part of me, and when they both stepped back, I turned around to run back again and kill the motherfucker who had stabbed Carole, but saw him running for the second cab, which was just completing a U-turn, with blood streaming down his face.

But the driver drove into the wrong lane to get away from him, and shouting *"Espareme! Espareme!"* meaning "Wait for me! Wait for me!" he turned and started running in the same direction as the cab, still shouting, so he'd have enough speed to jump in when it passed, and I started running to cut him off, cussing under my breath, wanting to kill the motherfucker if I didn't do anything else, and he glanced back at me with his walleye and pounded on the fender as it passed him, pleading, *"Por favor! Por favor!"* and someone in the back seat threw open the door and grabbed his arm when they drew next to him and jerked him inside as the cab took off in a grinding second gear, and knowing I'd never catch up, I threw my mallet at it, while still running, watched it sail through the air and crash through the back window, splintering the glass, then slowed myself down and stopped and stood panting in the center of the road, watching the cab speed away, a blur of heads in the back seat, wishing, really wishing that I could have caught the cat and beat him to death, then suddenly remembered Carole and ran across the road and jumped down into the ditch, but almost landed on her since she had moved, was higher up now and doubled up on her side, headed toward the roadway as if she had tried to climb out of the ditch while I was still fighting.

"Carole! Carole!" I cried, hoping that she might still be alive, and rolled her gently over on her back.

But her face was a deep red, her eyes perfectly motionless, her mouth open and still, and there was a spreading blood spot in the green chiffon between her breasts.

8

TEARS FILLED MY EYES, SPILLED OUT
and ran down my cheeks when I saw the blood spot
between her breasts where the blade must have slid
in just under the rib cage and killed her. But my
nose filled up quickly and I had to breathe through
my mouth and my sobbing could hardly be heard
because of my heavy breathing: almost no voice at
all, no wailing tone to it, mostly the sound of my
fast breath coming from deep down in my chest like
it hurt, and the sniffing back of mucus in my nose.

Her pale eyes hurt me the most, though, because
they looked so normal, a little glazed and motionless, but without any kind of stare in them, as if
she were only daydreaming. But the tip of her tongue
showed in her open mouth, against her bottom teeth,
and bothered me too, and I remembered a Spanish
woman who had tied her American husband's jaw
closed with a bandanna in Mexico City after he died
from a heart attack, and I looked around me for
something to tie Carole's mouth closed with and
saw her dark green scarf lying in the dust by Sam's
feet as if she had dropped it in her hurry to get out
of the car door.

I glanced at Sam's face as I stepped back and bent

down to pick it up, saw how tight his lips were, how hollowed his eyes looked in his dusty face, staring down at Carole but still standing by the door as if he was going to get back in the car, but ignored him, picked up the scarf and turned around, then kneeled down, and, holding it by both ends, hooked it under her jaw and up both sides of her face to the top of her head without touching her with my hands and was glad of that. But when I pulled her jaw up it clicked mechanically, and I winced, though I forced myself to tie the knot at the top of her head anyway, catching some long strands of her blond hair in it, then forced myself to close her eyes with the tips of my fingers too, but winced again when I felt the eyeballs under the lids. A sob welled up with some tears then and I squeezed my eyes shut until the wave passed over me, then blinked to clear the tears from them and heard a peddler cry out close by, looked up with blurry vision for a moment, and then stood up and looked around.

Nearly all the Mexicans were in the cab already—I could see well from my place in the ditch—and the two guys who hadn't been hit were helping the cab-driver into the back seat, where the dude was already sitting, slumped down, and with his white hat either back on or still on, next to the young kid, who was slumped down too, but who seemed to be alert, though aching some I'd bet. And I was glad that the mallet was small, not more than ten inches from the top of the brass to the bottom of the handle, and that I hadn't killed anybody, though I wondered why not. I had tried to.

The two guys, who both had on relatively new

work clothes—you could still see the original blue color of them—got into the front seat by themselves, and one of them started the motor, put the cab in gear, gunned the motor to get full power, and with it wide open, dug out like a race driver and shot past me at high speed, as if he was afraid I was going to try and stop them or something, though he was wrong, and I caught a good look at the dude, who looked back with a vague kind of expression on his face, pinching at a pimple, then quickly disappeared with the cab into the violet shadows of the dry hills.

In the opposite direction, the sun was a beautiful flame-color and was just about to set above the coastal hills by the border and was so weak I could look right into it. But the line of American cars was almost to the spot where the cab had been and both lanes of the highway were being used now, making a double line of backed-up cars, and I wondered where they had all come from, since not very many had come down the highway when I was fighting or before the fight for that matter. Though a lot of them were passing slowly by now, their moving shadows stretching completely across the ditch, the passengers inside them staring down at us, they still were not about to stop and take a chance on helping us like the Mexicans had helped each other.

The air was fresher, though, and a slight breeze was cooling the sweat on my face, drying the tear streaks; my breath was almost normal; no heavy rise and fall of my chest, but I glanced down at Carole again and another hot wave of tears came up, blurring her body below me, and I had to take a deep breath and then hold it to stifle the sobs until the wave passed, then I turned around to Sam.

He was still standing in the same spot, still staring down at Carole. But I saw the roll of brown bombers in his blue-stained fingers and realized that he had never let go of them to help me fight or to protect her, and I stepped down to him, measuring his jaw, ready to blast him for letting the guy kill her, wanting to punish *someone* for her death and expecting him to show fear of me. But he didn't even look at me, not even when I stood in front of him, stared straight ahead with hollowed eyes and that's all. So I snatched the roll out of his hand, glared at him to see if he wanted to do anything about it and hoped he would. But when he still didn't move, I leaned back to throw it out in the field, do that at least, mad at the grass too for being the cause of all the trouble in the first place, for being dope, and to clean up for when the cops came besides, because they were coming.

But I saw his face when I raised my arm to throw, and his mouth started working as if he was trying to say something to me but couldn't get the words out, and suddenly worn out, with no more fight left in me, feeling as responsible for her death as he was, I said, "Fuck it," and dropped my arm, said, "Fuck it," again and leaned against the car next to him, not capable of getting mad at anyone, not even him, and even warned: "It'll be dark in just a minute or two, Sam, and not one of those American cars is going to stop and give us a hand, and I can't say I blame them. But those Mexican cats—even if they don't want to get involved—will get a cop to come and get us, throw us in jail for a while. Somebody will report this. So unless you want to do some dead-time, waiting around for investigation of murder, you better get going, man."

My voice welled up with self pity over his not helping me and maybe saving her, and he finally spoke, asking, "What are *you* going to do?"

"Wait here for them." I met his gaze directly so he'd know I meant it. "I can't drive my car out of this ditch anyway. It would be a waste of time to try it. And I'm not running anymore besides. I'm tired of it. I've done it once too often now. I'm not going down to Mazatlán or anyplace else but San Francisco when they let me cross that border again."

"San Francisco might want you for being involved in that murder in the Haight, man!" he said, his voice rising as he spoke, like he was finally beginning to understand what I meant, what I was warning him about.

"I don't care," I said. "I didn't kill him technically and I didn't kill her technically, but I had something to do with both deaths, and I'm not running anymore. I'm tired of it. I'm going to face both charges."

"They'll try to hang you in both countries, man," he said and stepped clear of the door, up higher in the ditch to face me, with a worried squint to his deep-set eyes.

"I'll get me a lawyer and maybe even ask my old man to help me, and I won't answer a question until I get on the stand. But I'm not going to run anymore. Look what it's done to Carole. And besides, I can't just run off and leave her, man. I've got to do something with her body.''

We both looked at her again. Little flecks of deep shadow checked the hollows of dust around her legs, which she had spread for me the night before, but which were stiff and angular now, all knees and thin shanks, and tears welled up hot in my eyes again, and I shook my head at myself for being such a cry-baby, but didn't try to stop it, and Sam said, "Hey, man. You're really suffering," and reached down and grabbed my shoulder.

"It's O.K., man," I said, "Don't sweat it. It'll go right away. Give me a match and I'll light up a joint."

I pulled a bomber out of the roll and flicked both ends loose, stuck it in my mouth to wet it so it would burn slowly, but sobbed when I opened my mouth, and another wave of tears came up, and I had to jerk the joint out of my mouth and hand it to Sam, then fight back the tears by holding my breath, my chest aching.

He stuck the joint in his mouth and struck a light in his cupped hands, then made a zigzag motion with the flame as he reached out and touched my arm, smiled to make me feel better, and lifted the flame to his mouth to light the fat joint, the stick wheezing with flame when he sucked air in, the bony highlights of his cheeks and brows, his dark eyes glowing red as he took three deep tokes, then handed the joint to me.

I toked up on three deep hits without letting any air out or taking any in between the tokes, but took so much I had to suck in a whole mouthful of air and hold it to keep the smoke down and keep from coughing, and the cries of the peddlers sounded thin and flat against the motor drone of the American cars that stretched in both lanes as far as our stalled MG now. I gave the joint back to him, but the grass got to me fast and before we were through with the joint, my mouth was dry and furry, full of cotton; that is, my tongue was probably covered with little, white, saliva specks which often happens with good weed, and everything around me seemed peaceful, even pleasant. The idling motors of the tourists' cars had a sleepy sound and the cricket-cricket-cricket noise lulled my senses as I lazily watched Sam tear a matchbook cover off and start rolling it into a crutch to use as a cigarette holder for the roach of the joint when a peddler appeared just above us, his arms loaded with blankets and sandals, ready to try and sell us something. But he dropped back as if somebody had thrown a punch at him when he saw Carole, stared at me and Sam for a moment more and then stepped back onto the pavement and disappeared as if he had never seen us, and I didn't blame him.

"Sam," I said. "You better take off down that highway too or go hide in the town or take a bus out of it or something, if you don't want to get busted with me."

"Don't I have time, man?" he asked, his small eyes sagging heavily like the weed had already gotten to him too.

"No, you don't," I said and took another toke off the roach, then with my chin tucked in and my voice squeaking out because I didn't want to lose any smoke, I said, "They'll grab you off that highway fast if they start looking for you. There aren't many cars going east at night. Go on, split. There's no need for you to stay. She's my chick. Take the roll, too. Just leave me another joint to smoke while I'm waiting for them."

There wasn't any bitterness to my voice and he took the roll from me and gave me back a joint but had a frown on his face that puzzled me, and I said, "Get going, man."

But he stood there looking down on me, frowning, and asked, "Don't you care if you're locked up?" And when I shook my head, he almost said something, but then shook his head too while still staring at me, then squatting down, pulled another joint out of the roll, struck a match and lit it up, like if I didn' care, he didn't care very much either.

There was a small crack of a popping seed which somebody had missed when they cleaned the grass, followed by a tiny stream of billowing smoke out of the end of the joint as he sucked in deep, and I couldn't help but admire the way he stuck around and took a chance on jail now that I was willing to go there without fighting anymore. He was evidently true to his Eastern philosophy of passive acceptance of all things, good and bad, since they all added up to a complete whole in the end anyway, and I wondered if I'd be able to write in jail, both the Mexican and the American ones I was going to inhabit, and whether I'd be so calm myself after they slammed those iron doors on me. Which might be soon. It was getting late.

WHAT NOW MY LOVE

Most of the cars in the double line had their lights on now that the sun had gone down and the moon was up and bright, just an inch or two above the dark hills in the east, reflecting off the flat roofs of the low buildings of the town behind us in white patches. The lights of the town were bright too and thousands and thousands of American cars were strung across the fields from the town to the border in bright strings, revealing to me how very many roads crossed those fields and how the line of jammed cars had gotten so long so quickly. The border was itself a mass of lights at the base of the coast hills to the northwest of us.

But Carole's blond hair glowed in the moonlight, too, and the tears rose up to my eyes again and blurred all the lights, and I wasn't sure whether or not I saw a cowboy hat bob up by a car light a few cars down the road. But when I blinked my eyes to clear them and the hat bobbed up by the next car too, coming my way, and was followed by the squat figure of another man, who was vaguely familiar, both of them with their faces turned toward the ditch as if they were looking for us, I said, "Here comes that pimple-faced, cowboy dude again and with the cop who almost busted me today, Sam." I knew the other guy was the cop just because the dude knew him. "You better take off down the ditch right now or he'll bust you."

Sam stood up and blocking the glare from the headlights with his hand tried to see down the highway, then dropped his hand, turned back around, looked at me long and carefully, and, apparently satisfied that I wasn't scared, stepped back by the

car and pulled another joint out of the roll and lit
it, without saying anything, though I noticed that
the match flame trembled and that he had a little
trouble getting the joint started. Still, he didn't run
and we were both standing there, leaning against
the car, smoking our bombers when the dude and
the cop stopped in the headlight glare at the top of
the ditch and stared down at us.

"You looking for me?" I asked, and the dude
jabbed his finger at me and rattled off something in
Spanish to the cop, then stepped back on the shoulder
to let the cop go first and said something else, and I
figured that the tall hat had softened the blow of the
mallet, brass was soft anyway, or the guy wouldn't
have been able to walk around, to come back and
find us with the cop.

"Whot?" the bull asked, his teeth bright under
his black mustache, though his squat back was to the
headlights, then said, "Shot op!" speaking to the
guy in English both times, which surprised me.
Then, with the dude following him, stirring up
little clouds of dust that flared momentarily white
in the headlights, he came heavily down into the
ditch, stopped in front of us, looked at me, arched
his heavy brow and nodded his head as if he knew
it all the time, glanced once at Sam, and asked,
"You guys smoking weed?" When I nodded, he
stepped up to Carole, eased himself down, seemed to
pick a less dusty spot for his knee, and looked at
her, but had to drop his head even then to get his
eyes below the beam of the headlights and see her
well.

The lights still cut her body off from my sight,

thankfully, cast a not quite transparent sheen of white over the darkness where she lay, and I forced myself to concentrate, in order to keep myself from staring at her, on all the gear shifting and motor rapping, the billow and stink of exhausts, the red blink of taillights, as the lane near me moved up a couple of spaces with a rippling jerk that went out of sight down the highway.

"Is that your car?" the bull asked, and when I nodded, he said, "Help me put her inside."

Sticking my half-smoked bomber in a corner of my mouth, I stepped up in the ditch above her and bent down to help without any qualms. But when I grabbed her under the arms, I dropped the joint out of my mouth and started to cry again, and the tears blurred everything so badly, with the bright lights glaring from one side, that I couldn't even see her. Then my nose filled up and I had to breathe through my mouth, which made a little sobbing noise, and the cop, who was just lifting her up on her stiffened legs, looked at me with a surprised frown that I could even see through my tears, like he never expected sobs from a guy who just beat the shit out of a gang of Mexicans with a brass mallet over a little burn, and who could talk himself out of a bust. But I picked her up anyway to let him know that I wasn't going to break down, tears or not, and he lifted up her legs and told the dude something in Spanish about opening the door, and the guy lifted the edge of the door out of the dust and forced it open a foot or two more so we could get in with her body.

"Me first," I said and moved in a circle around

the cop so that I could get into the car with most of
her weight before him, though I had to knock the
back of the bucket seat down with my knee before
I could slip into the back seat. I eased her past the
steering wheel, forced the gearshift out of high into
neutral with her hip, and rested her back against
the door, her body tilted my way, her hair hanging
over the back of the seat like it had when I cupped
my hand over her crotch the night before, and tears
misted my eyes again. But I slipped back out the
driver's side without sobbing or looking at her
again, then stood in the ditch next to Sam and the
cop.

But the dude started chattering in Spanish again
and waving his hands in the air and pointing at me,
the peak of his hat a cone of light, as if he still might
be a little groggy from the whack on the head that
I'd given him. I had seen professional fighters who
had been knocked out not come around again until
the next day, though they had been walking and
talking and acting normal in nearly every other way.
The guy was really excited, though, and seemed to
be trying to get the cop to beat me up or something.
The cop argued with him over his shoulder for a
moment, the tips of his mustache as thin as antennae
in the glare of the lights that whitened his face, then
shrugged finally and turning to me, pulled his small
automatic out of his shoulder holster and showed it
to me to scare me, I guess.

But he didn't. I just looked at the gun and then
at him. We knew each other better than that by
now. But Sam stuck his long arms straight up in the
air, and he was tall, with the lighted joint in one

hand and the roll of bombers in the other, his eyes bright as an animal's with fear, and I couldn't help grinning. The cop saw that too and quickly said, "Put your arms down. Don't be a fool," then stuck his gun back in his shoulder holster and spun around and straight-armed the dude in the chest, knocked him into a sitting position in the ditch above him, and, though the dude's arms flew up, his hat stayed on, and he crawled up the ditch a few feet out of the bull's striking range before he dared to stand up again, and kept quiet.

"How much money you got?" the bull asked. "And tell me the truth or I'll shake you down and take it all away from you."

"About ten bucks," I said and looked hard at Sam so he'd lie and hold on to his two grand. He squinted his eyes like he understood me, but when the cop glared at him hard too, he suddenly said, "Two thousand," and the cop grinned, then, very serious again, said to me:

"How about the girl?" and broke into another grin, the points of his mustache curling up, when I answered, "Four hundred," giving up altogether since Sam had copped out, and not caring either. Fuck the money. Fuck it all, especially when the cop, very serious again, let us know where we stood.

"If I decide to lock you guys up for investigation," he said and stared up at Sam to keep him scared, "you'll have to stay in jail until it's over, and that might take two or three years."

"We didn't kill her," Sam said, really worried, going for the shuck story right away.

"I know you didn't. But this guy here," the cop

said and jabbed his thumb at me. "He almost killed four Mexicans—the cabdriver's in the hospital with broken ribs, and the Mexican government don't like Americans coming down here and beating up their people. So they stretch the investigation out until you pay a big 'fee' through an expensive lawyer. Understand?"

Sam's mouth dropped open and he looked at me to see what I thought, but I looked at the cop and nodded, waiting for him to say how much, since he could take it all anyway, and he did, saying, "I'll take your two thousand, the girl's four hundred, and you, I'll take your car, and you can split the ten between you. Either that or I take you both to jail for investigation of murder, and there's no bail in Mexico. Remember that. What do you say?"

"How about her body? Will her family get her body?" I asked and had to stop talking because another of those hot tear waves seemed to come up from out of my tight belly. I wouldn't cry in front of the guy, though I had to lower my head and close my eyes until it passed.

He stood in front of me without answering until I raised my head again and then said, "Yes," in an understanding way that was so considerate of my feelings that I had to look down again and catch my breath to keep the tears back. But I was looking right at the spot where she had been lying, and I said out loud: "Carole. I helped kill you in my way. And I'll see that you get to a grave. But I'm not going to do two or three years dead-time over your corpse." Then I wiped my eyes with my fingers and said to Sam: "He can have my car, man. I'm going back across that border to San Francisco and face what's up there waiting for me. I've had it in Mexico. What are you going to do?"

Sam stood there for a moment with his face sticking up high above me, a scared-looking white in the headlights, his deep-set eyes glittering with reflections under his brows. Then he flipped the joint away, put his hand in his pocket, pulled out the wad of marked money, and, still holding the roll of joints in his other hand, peeled off three or four small bills, handed the roll of hundreds to the cop, and said, "That's two thousand." Then he turned to me and added in a confident voice: "I'm going to hitchhike down to Mazatlán and see my friends."

The dude started chattering before I got a chance to show Sam that I liked the way he kept the small bills, and came down the ditch to get a closer look at the money wad. But the bull raised his thick arm like he was going to backhand him, and the dude cowered down and backed up a few steps, then the cop turned to me and holding out his hand, asked for my keys.

"They're in the back," I said, pointing. "Can I get my personal stuff out of there and get going?"

He hesitated before answering, like he might be thinking of keeping everything of mine, but then wrinkled up his mustache and nodded, and I stepped to the back of the car, stuffed my sleeping bag and briefcase in my duffel bag, since there weren't very many clothes in it, then clipped the mouth of the duffel bag together, slung it by its strap over my shoulder, shifted it a little bit to get the weight comfortable, then grabbed my typewriter with my free hand and said, *"Adíos,"* to the bull, who answered politely. But I ignored the dude, though I could see him well until I stopped at the top of the ditch, where I said, "So long," to Sam, who waved and started up the ditch in the opposite direction, looking at me curiously, his face in shadow, until he reached the roadway too, where he waved again and started hiking down the shoulder toward Mazatlán, a thousand miles distant.

The border was a bunch of lights and vague dark shapes about five or six miles ahead of me, which I made the mistake of thinking was closer because of a curve in the road that shortened the seeing distance but not the walking distance and which I didn't even know was in the road until I reached it and saw how much further I still had to go. The strap of the duffel bag cut into my shoulder, too, as soon as I started, it was made so heavy by the briefcase, which was full of manuscripts and typing paper, a few books, but it didn't slow me down and shifting it from shoulder to shoulder helped ease it a lot. The car lights didn't bother me at all because I walked in the same direction in which they were beamed, and even losing my car didn't make much difference to me. It was better to lose it than go to jail for an investigation which would have ended up with my having to give it away for a bribe anyway after doing months of dead-time first, and then being shipped back to San Francisco besides. And I wasn't about to go on down into Mexico with Sam and his measly fifty or so dollars, where anything could have happened to me, and nobody would have even known about it. So heading back to San Francisco and all the trouble I might get into up there didn't shake me up much either. But Carole did.

I cried and didn't give a fuck who saw me, not the peddlers nor the people in the cars, especially not the people in the cars. I fought the bitterness that I felt toward them. People from my own country who wouldn't so much as roll down a window and shout for help if they saw a Mexican try to kill me in front of them. People who supported the laws that made dope illegal in America and forced people like Sam and Carole and I into the underworld, helped kill her and made an outlaw of me, had made my life since I started smoking pot with my older brother's suicide ten years before a pariah's misery, in fact.

Bitterness didn't help me feel any better though, and when I finally rounded the curve in the road that had confused me about the distance and was close enough to the border gate to read the Standard sign of the service station just inside the Mexican border, I figured I'd better quit feeling sorry for myself and start thinking about what I was going to say to the guard when I got to the gate. And this took my mind off my sorrow for a while.

But the cries of the hundreds and hundreds of Mexican peddlers who hustled the tourists' cars that bunched up together in the huge, paved clearing about the size of a city block in front of the gate, and the general din of the car motors, the exhaust raps, the grinding gears, the horn honks by impatient drivers, the bright lights that I had to pick my way through, skipping hurriedly out of the way of a car once in a while after one had bumped my leg because the driver was in such a big hurry to move up a half a space, all took out of my mind even my plan to say that I got left behind by some buddies, out of my mind, and I didn't even get another chance to think about what I'd say at all until I finally reached the sidewalk line for footcrossers at one side of the carports and had to wait my turn to pass by the brown-uniformed guard, who was questioning briefly each guy who stepped in front of him, and who were mostly sailors from San Diego both in and out of uniform.

My hands started sweating so badly now that I was just about to cross back over the border—even though I knew I had nothing to fear from the guard since I was going back to San Francisco and all my troubles anyway, and the most he could do was throw me in jail—that I had to put my duffel bag and typewriter down on the sidewalk and wipe my palms on my cords several times. And I was just putting my gear down to wipe my hands for about the tenth time when the sailor in front of me passed through the gate and the guard turned his clean-shaven face toward mine below him, let his pale blue eyes rest on it, and I saw Carole's blue eyes, not his, flash up out of the ditch at me.

Shocked, I stood up too fast, wide-eyed with the hallucination, dizzy, my whole head buzzing, and my sight blurred so badly with the wave of tears that misted my eyes that all the lights around me, his face, her eyes, shimmered out of focus. Afraid I was going to faint, I ducked my head down again to let the blood come back to it and to hide it from him, stalled that way as if I were having trouble picking up my stuff until my face got warm with blood again and my eyesight cleared. Then I whispered good-by to her for the last time and straightened up once more, slung my duffel bag over my shoulder, picked up my typewriter, and stepped forward into his blue-eyed stare, ready to answer his questions and go back to America and nothing.